AF480699

Bane

K.J. Dahlen

K.J. Dahlen
Bane

Book Design, Editing & Formatting: Wicked Muse[1]
Cover Art Provided By: Cosmic Letterz[2]

---

1. https://www.facebook.com/bonnie.l.elliott.7/

2. https://www.facebook.com/CosmicLetterz/

Prologue

A year ago...

Bane gave the dark a cold grin. Oh yeah, this would be fun for him. He hated playing games with people's lives, but this was a game he knew he would win.

He'd just climbed a tree outside Stark's compound. He'd traveled here during daytime hours and using the trees as cover, he scoped out the place. He didn't dare get too close, as he didn't want Stark to have any clue he was being watched. He'd used the cover of shadows to get where he wanted to be. He also knew he wasn't alone in these woods. He couldn't see anyone, but he knew they were there all the same. He felt them waiting while watching him and the clubhouse.

Checking his watch, he noted the time. He had a few hours left before Deke said he would come for the MC.

Some of Stark's men were milling around the clubhouse, making all the noise they wanted. They had no clue anyone was out there, either that or they just didn't care. Bane brought his hand crafted rifle equipped with a silencer up to his shoulder and took out three men. They dropped without a word or a sound.

Bane took out another four men before Stark even noticed they were missing. When he found his men dead, he panicked and closed his clubhouse up, finally taking up a fighting position behind its closed doors. He barricaded what was left of his men and they just began shooting at anything that moved outside. They are at a stalemate right now.

Bane knew time was running out and decided to stir things up a bit. He laid down on the branch holding him and took the shot. A moment later, the fuel tank blew up. A second later, the clubhouse blew up as well. Bane sat up and grinned slightly.

Screams and chaos echoed around him.

Bane slid down the tree and began breaking down his weapon. He was going to walk away when a shot rang out. He felt the bite of pain that hit him. Gasping he turned, grabbing the handgun at his waist and fired instinctively.

Stark had stumbled from the burning house and had seen Bane walking away. He got one shot off and Bane had been hit but Bane turned around and literally smoked Stark. The shot took him completely off his feet. He flew back about five feet before he hit the ground. Then he didn't move again. His dead eyes stared at the canopy of stars overhead. His clothes were still smoking from the burning building he'd just stumbled out of.

Bane turned wordlessly and walked deeper in the woods. At this point, he could no longer feel the pain of the gunshot but he could feel the blood pouring down his side. He knew he was going into shock and there was nothing he could do to stop it. The bullet caught him in the back shoulder and came out in his upper chest.

Each step he took, he knew he was growing weaker from blood loss. He sat down when he was far enough away from the crime scene. Leaning his head against the tree, he just felt tired.

He thought about the events of the night. Cricket getting married when she thought she only had another day to live. It had astounded him at the time.

When he'd walked into the Sin's Bastard's clubhouse earlier tonight before all of this, he took in the flowery arch, the candles, and the sense of pure happiness. Then he saw Cricket's face and he had to stop and stare at her for a moment.

She'd looked so much like her mother. Her hair was a little different, but her eyes were exactly like his Grace. The only difference was Grace never once looked at him the same way Cricket was looking at Raine. Grace's eyes never held for him the emotion Cricket had in hers at the moment. Grace's eyes only held pain and fear for him.

The noise level dropped so suddenly, it took him a moment to hear it. Then he glanced around the room.

"Raine and I just got married." Cricket pushed her way around Raine's huge body to face her uncle.

"Married?" Bane frowned. "You got married? At this hour?"

Cricket nodded. "I was born at this time of the day twenty-four years ago. With our present situation, Raine wanted to give me something special for my birthday."

When he turned to leave, Cricket called out, "Uncle, would you like to stay and celebrate with us?"

Bane turned around slowly to stare at her. "I don't celebrate. But enjoy your moment. Happiness rarely lasts very long." He looked over at Deke. "Those other two men you were looking for earlier? I found them once but they got away. They may not make it very far but they got away from me." He shook his head. "I must be getting old. I never should have missed them."

Then he disappeared through the door.

He had wondered at the time...What the bloody hell was wrong with her? What the hell was wrong with him? Why had she taken that moment to ask him to stay? Why had he almost stayed? He realized now that this girl was Grace's daughter after all. He saw in her what it was that touched him the first time he'd seen her mother.

Now, he was satisfied that Stark would no longer be a threat to Cricket. She had proven herself to him and to the rest of the world. He didn't have to worry about her anymore. He knew the MC would take care of her.

He smiled faintly as he thought about what he'd done tonight. He had taken out an entire MC. His last act on this earth had been protecting a woman who hated him, one who wanted nothing to do with him. Hell, she didn't even want the name she should have been born with. She was a true Jessin and she didn't want that title.

Jessin was a name to be proud of even if she didn't want it. That name would be gone forever now. He had no children left to carry the name, even his grandson would have a different name by now.

Then he thought about what he'd placed on the front seat of his car. He wanted Cricket to know that he knew about the boy Dusty. She needed to know that he knew, yet he hadn't done anything to claim the boy.

His will was there as well. He knew he might now live through this and he was right. Stark had gotten one good shot off before he met his Maker, whether he went to heaven or hell it didn't matter any longer. Bane had put out the trash, as Deke would have said. He grinned at the irony of it all. Deke would have considered him trash as well, he didn't doubt that one bit.

Cricket and Dusty would be safe now. At least he'd done that much for them. He tried to get up but lacked the strength to do so. Instead, he just sat there and thought about what Cricket would do when she heard he was dead. He knew there was always the chance that tonight could be his last night on this earth.

The sad part of his life was he had nothing to show for his existence. Oh, he had money and a sort of frame but anybody could have those things. He had a big house and nice cars and expensive art works on his walls but again those were just material things. That was cold comfort in the end.

He had tried a wife and family but that hadn't worked out for him either. He felt something strange trailing down his cheeks and he frowned and raised a hand to brush it off his face.

His hand came away wet but there was no color to the wetness. Was he crying? Were those actual tears running down his cheeks? How strange, Bane thought. Never in his fifty-seven years had he cried. Not even as a child and he'd been hurt.

Now in his last few moments of life he was crying. Bane didn't understand why.

He wasn't afraid of dying. It was a natural progression of things he couldn't control. You were born, you grew up and hopefully you lived a good long life then you died.

He had missed out on so much and until now, it never bothered him. He had gone through life with no real feelings of any kind, but he hadn't known regret until now. His lack of feeling hadn't bothered him either.

His only real regret now that he thought about it had been not making Grace love him. He regretted the fact that even if she had stayed with him there hadn't been a chance of her loving him, not the same way she loved Orrin. Only now did he realize you couldn't force someone to love you, that kind of feeling cannot be forced. If it's meant to be, it will be. All those years ago, he tried forcing her and it hadn't worked.

He and Orrin had been as different as day and night. Orrin had feelings, he knew what it was like to fly high or drop so low you had to claw your way up just to breathe the air you needed to survive.

He'd been there when Grace had his daughter, Cordy and he'd been there when Grace went through labor to bring his own daughter into this world. He'd also been there when Grace breathed her last breath. Orrin had grieved for Grace every day after that until the day Cordy blew him up.

He raised his teary eyes to the heavens and called out, "I'm sorry brother. I never understood what you went through. I dropped the ball with Grace. I missed out on having a family I so desperately wanted with her, but you didn't. I made your life a living hell and until now I didn't understand why I did that." Hanging his head, he said, "I know it too little too late, but I saved your girl tonight. I took out a threat to her life and I'm glad I did that. I want you and Grace to know that I forgive you. I know I didn't say the words when it could have made a difference, but I am sorry. I put the blame on your shoulders when it should have been on mine all along."

He tipped his head back and stared at the stars overhead. "I know you and Grace are together in heaven and I envy you that. My children and my enemies are waiting in hell for me to join them and I deserve that. The Jessin line ends tonight and that's the way it should be. You told me that a very long time ago but I was too arrogant to listen, too full of my own expectations to care what you thought. I thought I had time to have a son of my own to carry on the name I was so proud to bear."

He coughed and couldn't stop. Each cough brought him fresh pain and he could feel a gush of fresh blood pumping out of the hole in his chest. When he was finally able to catch his breath, Bane felt his head swimming. Everything around him was floating and he had spots behind his eyelids.

Bane wasn't ready to give up the fight just yet. "Grace," he whispered, "Please forgive me for being who I was when I knew you. I did care about you but I didn't know how to treat you back then. I hurt you time and time again when I should have cherished you. You never betrayed me and I could face that now. I betrayed you. It took your sweet daughter to teach me that. I only wish I could redo my life. I got too good at killing and not very good at living. I should have surrounded my life with living not with death and dying. Now it's too late for that and hell is coming for me."

Tears dried on his face as he faced his final goodbye. "Grace, Orrin, please forgive me," he whispered as he felt his heartbeat slow down. He didn't try and fight the inevitable.

Suddenly, the silence surrounding him was broken by the sound of footsteps and then someone walked out of the shadows.

Bane raised the gun that was still in his hand and pointed it at the man walking toward him.

This didn't stop the man, he didn't even hesitate in his steps. Instead, he came right up to where Bane was sitting and squatted next to him.

"Who the fuck are you and what do you want here?" Bane finally asked.

"They call me many names but most people know me as the Priest."

Bane growled. "You're too late if killing me is on your mind. Stark's bullet took care of that."

Priest shook his head. "I didn't come here to kill you, but instead to ask you a question."

Bane raised an eyebrow. "And what would that be?"

"I want to ask you if you want a do over?"

"A do-over? Is there such a thing for men like us?" Bane had to ask.

"There could be if you want it bad enough."

Bane snorted. "No one ever gets the chance for a life do over."

"Then you don't want it bad enough." He started to stand up.

Bane reached out and grabbed his arm pulling him back down. "Why? Why would you offer me something like this? What's in for you?"

Priest shrugged. "Not a goddamn thing. Men like you and me? We know fifty ways to kill another man but we don't know squat about living. We don't know anything about why other people find love but we never could."

"You don't know me." Bane growled.

"I know more about you than you think. I never thought I was worthy of a better life either, then I met the real person I was meant to be. The man I never dared to dream I could be. When I found out about this mission I had to come and offer you the same chance I was given. It was scary as hell and I feared nothing. But I took that step and I'll never regret what I did. I'm here to either watch you give up and die or take the chance and learn to live. The thing is if you take that chance you have to walk away from your old life. No more killing. Can you do that? Can you give up everything you've worked a lifetime to gain?"

Bane thought about that for a moment then nodded. "I'd sure like to try."

Priest reached out his hand and Bane slowly accepted it. Hauling him to his feet, Priest threw his arm around the injured man and led him back to the shadows. They passed another man hauling a dead body to the place Bane had rested.

Bane turned and watched as the other man propped the dead man up against the tree.

He stripped off the Dragon's MC cut from his shoulder and reached for the weapon Bane had dropped. Pointing it at the other man's face, he pulled the trigger and in an instant, the other man's face exploded. Blood and debris flew everywhere but there was nothing left to identify the body against the tree.

Then another shot rang out. The second man got up, walked into the shadows to bring out another body, and threw it to the ground.

It was Stark's body.

Then he joined Priest and Bane.

Priest smiled slightly. "That's step one."

"Step one?" Bane asked.

"Toward the end of your old life, now we have to set up your recovery and the beginning of your new life."

Chapter One

A year later... Troy, New York

Theo Franks sat at the café with his companion Sarah and was having a cup of coffee when Cricket, Reva and Cassie walked by. Theo looked carefully at his niece and about choked on the sip of coffee he just had. Coffee sprayed all over the table and him, including in his beard.

Cricket was pushing a baby stroller in front of her, a baby stroller meant to hold more than one child.

His eyes narrowed as he thought back to a year ago. Had she been pregnant then or was this an after effect to the rush of danger she'd been in then? He watched as the women stopped long enough for Reva to pick up one of the fussy babies inside the stroller. Then he saw Cassie pick up another squalling baby and still Cricket rocked the stroller, as if there was a third child in there.

Theo felt stunned at what was right in front of him. From the size of the babies, he knew they were a few months old. Had she already been pregnant when he saw her last?

Sarah looked over at him in concern. "Are you all right?"

Theo wiped his mouth and nodded. "Yeah, I'm fine." He turned to watch the three women as they crossed the street at the corner.

Sarah leaned forward and placed her hand over his. "Do you know those people?"

Theo stared at Cricket for a long moment then turned to face Sarah. "Yeah, I know one of them anyway, from my past."

He was no longer the man he'd been a year ago. At least he no longer looked like the same man. But he knew that just changing his face didn't necessarily change the man he'd once been. But he was working on that. He was still tall, dark-haired with hazel eyes but his face wasn't the same. But it was more than just the shape of his face, now he had a full beard covering his scars from the surgeries he'd had.

His body was no longer as slim as it once was either. Now his muscles were taut and his body reveled in his strength. He might have been an older man but it didn't show. He'd been rebuilding his body as well as his soul this last year.

"Why did we come here?" Sarah asked him.

He felt annoyed for a moment then shook off the feeling. She had a right to ask him that. He thought about how they met. Sarah was the first person he'd seen when he'd come around after his reconstructive surgery.

The Priest had taken him to a private clinic in Bath, Maine. A doctor there had put him in a medically induced coma to recover the surgery necessary to recover from the bullet wound he'd gotten from Stark. He had arrived half dead due to blood loss and the coma was the only way he could get the medical help he needed to live.

Those first few weeks had been touch and go for Bane. He hadn't been aware of any of it though as the doctor kept him knocked out long enough to see if he would live or die. When he recovered enough to be moved, they took him to a private clinic for more recovery. Finally, three months after the shooting, he had recovered enough to wake up from his medical induced sleep.

As Priest told him the next few months weren't easy, but they had been necessary. Taking it slow and easy, he endured three separate surgeries to transform his face.

While he recovered from that, he'd seen a plastic surgeon about reconstructing his looks. He would still be who he always was but with a new face, he could become whoever he wanted to be. Priest had told him he would have to give up his past and work on becoming a new person and he had. When he finally walked out of that damn clinic, Bane Jessin was nothing more than a memory. He'd walked out as Theo Orlan Franks. Priest had built him a new life, providing a new background and legal records to prove who he was.

But with everything he'd done, he was still a work in progress. He could have ignored the rumors he'd heard, ignored the threat that was coming and just let the chips fall where they may, but then Cricket had done something that made no sense to him.

She had buried what she thought was his body. He had to wonder why after all he'd put her through, why she would do that. He hadn't expected that. He figured no one would step up and claim what was supposed to be his remains. But she had and she had buried him on the grounds of the compound.

Not only that but she hadn't wanted to take what he left for her. She hadn't ripped his home apart, selling his most prized possessions. She had only taken her father's blades back. The members of the MC had taken a few possessions, but they had left most of his things behind. Priest had bought his house and kept it in a trust for him. He'd been glad of that. That house had been the one thing he had left of his old life. That house held secrets and when he was able, he went to retrieve those secrets.

She had taken a good chunk of his money but again, she hadn't taken it all, only what she could carry. She had shared her fortune not only with Dusty but with the entire MC. He hadn't understood her actions but he was beginning to.

He looked over at Sarah. She was about 5 years older than Cricket and life had been hard for her. She shared bits and pieces of her life but she still had some secrets. Over the last twelve months, he'd grown close to her. He'd offered her the same choice given to him. A life do over. She'd been the one he woke up to that first day after the doctors brought him out of the coma.

Her touch was one he found he could tolerate. He'd never been able to stand being touched. He thought he found that with Grace but not even her touch calmed the beast inside him. But when Sarah touched him the beast calmed. He'd never had that before. The longer he was around her the more he needed her touch. They weren't lovers.

They were friends. He hadn't been ready all this time. He was still working on being a new man.

Over the last year, he had learned some about her but not everything. Her secrets she held deep inside her. Often, the nights he couldn't sleep they would sit up and talk, bits and pieces of their reflective pasts without revealing too much. He hadn't pushed her to divulge her secrets yet but he knew one day he would.

He was learning to trust again and that was something he'd never had before. Everyone in his life except for maybe his grandfather had betrayed him at some point but he didn't think Sarah would. She didn't know his secrets either. He found her presence comforting and was beginning to lean on her, to need her right beside him every day.

She told him Priest had contacted her to nurse him back to health. When he asked how she knew the man called Priest, all she would tell him was that she'd been in a bad place and he came to rescue her. They remained friends, although she didn't really know that much about him. When he called her to do him this favor, she came without hesitation.

When he asked her to accompany him here, she'd hesitated. Finally, she had admitted she didn't feel comfortable being here. It was too close to her past. A past she had yet to share with him. Bane told her he would protect her and she told him he'd better.

He decided to let a little bit of his past come out. He wanted to trust her with the truth about him. "Did you notice that woman with the stroller that just walked past us?" he asked.

Sarah nodded. "What about her?"

"She's my niece and she is the wife of a member of the local MC. I came here to warn the leader of that MC that trouble is coming his way. You see, seventeen years ago he killed a man that needed killing. Now the old president's brother and dad are finally out of prison and they are looking for Deke and seem to want to set right the wrong they feel was done to their kin. They want revenge for their brother and son and they don't care who they have to take out to get to Deke. I have a feeling this goes beyond Deke and that they want to wipe out the entire MC and just step into their lives here. They figure the Club belongs to them as deke killed the president years ago. Any threat to the MC is a possible threat to her and my grandson. I cannot and will not allow that."

"And what do you think you can do about it?" Sarah asked softly. "You can't stop them from coming."

"No I can't. But I can warn Deke and his boys that they're coming. At least I can give them that much."

"Why? Why would you do that?"

Bane thought about her question for a long time before he answered, "Not so long ago, I was a different man. We've talked a little about this over the year we've been together. The life I led was not one I care to even think about today but back then, my niece was willing to give her all for these men. I was back then, the kind of man that only took and took. She showed me another way altogether and I'm trying to be a better man."

"But honey, you can't go back. You can't always fix what you once broke." Sarah sighed. "Life doesn't work that way. You can regret things you've done in the past but you can't take back what you did."

Bane nodded. "I know. But she put her life on the line for them and she didn't have to do that. They didn't ask her to do that but she did anyway. They proved they were worthy of her sacrifice. She stood her ground and now it's my turn to prove I am worthy of what she did for them. What she did for me." He shrugged, "Maybe I just need to prove to myself that I have changed, that I can be worthy of her trust."

Sarah studied him for a moment then nodded. "Ok. I can understand that. So how are you going to approach this...them?"

Bane shrugged. "That's what I'm not sure of. They won't know the new me. I have to figure out a way to make contact with them without them remembering the man I once was. That man is gone and he has to stay gone. I can't go back to what I once was. This will be my test."

Just then, another man walked up to their table and sat down. He frowned at Bane and glared at Sarah pulling his sunglasses high on his head. "What the fuck are you doing here?"

Bane stared back. "I'm here to warn the MC about a man named Oscar Buckley."

"You shouldn't be here, it's too soon. Buckley isn't your concern or at least he shouldn't be," the Priest stated. "Why did you really come here?"

"That is a long story and I don't really want to sit here out in the open and explain it all to you." He had been picking up the feeling he was being watched. He casually looked around and caught the sight of an older man staring at their table.

Bane immediately knew he belonged to an MC. Maybe not any more but he had at one point. He looked casually over at Priest and said, "We're being watched and I don't like it."

Priest didn't look around but nodded. "Ok, let's go somewhere we can talk. Where is this man?"

"To your left, three tables away." Bane reached for his wallet to leave money for his and Sarah's coffee. He pulled out more than enough cash and dropped it on the table.

Sarah got to her feet and Priest stood up. Before he stepped away, he glanced over to the table Bane told him about and he clocked the man sitting there. He was staring at Bane, so Priest got a good look at him.

He saw the same thing Bane saw. The man was older and a past member of an MC.

He didn't make eye contact. Before they moved away, he covered his eyes with mirrored sunglasses and tapped his left bow.

They walked the two blocks to a hotel and went inside. They didn't hurry but instead walked casually so the two blocks took several minutes to traverse.

Priest led the way and they went up to the second floor to his room. Unlocking the door, he ushered Bane and Sarah inside. He turned and looked across the hall to the door opposite his own. It opened and a man appeared. The other man stepped out and handed him a piece of paper. The door closed again and Priest went inside his own room.

He took off the sunglasses and looked over at Bane. "Ok, what's going on and why did you come here? This was your past and I told you, you had to make a clean break with everything and everyone from your past in order to have a new life. You shouldn't be here."

"I came here to warn Deke about Oscar and Matty Buckley. They both just got out of prison in Maine and are looking for the man who killed Oscar's son, Dennis."

"Who killed him and why would Deke be interested in this news?"

"I've been running background checks on these guys. My niece Cricket and grandson Dusty live here and I want them to be safe. I found out seventeen years ago when Deke and his friends Gator and Reva came here and decided to stay, the President of the Satan's Spawn MC was a real bastard. His real name was Dennis Buckley, his road name was Bear and he gave the MC a bad name in this town."

Priest shrugged. "So what business is that here and now?"

"Deke shot and killed the man after he raped and stabbed a kid he took hostage. Then Deke took over the MC."

Priest shook his head. "Old man, you need to dig a little deeper. Deke didn't shoot Bear. Oh, he beat hell out of him but he didn't kill him. Not to say he wouldn't have but someone else pulled the trigger. His own VP, a man known as Breaker shot Bear before Bear could throw a knife at Deke's back."

Bane crossed his arms over his chest and glared at the other man. "I don't think Oscar and Matty will care who pulled the trigger. According to rumor, they left Maine three days ago. They both made comments that they were coming after the man who took the MC away from Bear."

Priest nodded. "I've been monitoring them too. I knew about this as well," he admitted. "They are hell bent for leather and taking no prisoners either. In fact, they aren't even trying to hide what they're doing. They want everyone in the biker world to know exactly what they're doing and why."

Bane looked at Sarah and frowned. "What exactly are they doing?"

"They are gathering all the old members of the MC, the ones that left when Deke took over, or rather the ones who are still alive. It has been a while, as you know. My contacts tell me they are raising hell along the way. They are building their own army of MC wannabe's. They want enough power behind them to take the MC back from Deke."

"How the hell are they going to do that?" Bane asked.

"They plan on walking over Deke's dead body right into the power positions. Anyone who doesn't like it will die right along with him. And that includes women and kids."

"Fucking hell…" Bane whispered.

Priest handed over the paper that his man across the hall had given him.

"What's this?" Bane asked as he took the paper.

"The man at the table in the café. His name is Kyle Ruppert, known as Breaker in the MC world."

"How the hell did you get this so fast? We just left the café?" Bane was stunned.

Priest smiled. "My man James. He's very fast and usually, right on the mark. We've been digging into the old MC, so we can identify the players. We've been looking into this since Oscar and Matty got out of prison. I was hearing the rumors while they were still inside." Priest sobered. "My question is what is Breaker doing here after all this time?"

"Maybe he heard the same rumors we did." Bane shrugged. "Why don't we find out?"

"Already ahead of you." Priest nodded. "James is bringing him to us."

Just then, a knock came at the door.

Priest walked over and looked through the peephole then quickly opened the door.

James ushered in a man sporting a few bruises and a split lip.

Breaker glared back at the man who pushed him into the room. "What the fuck do you people want with me? I ain't doing anything wrong."

"We only want answers, old man," Priest told him. "We aren't going to hurt you."

Breaker squinted as he judged if they were telling the truth or not. After a moment or so, he finally nodded. "What do you want to know?"

"Well for one, why did you leave the Satan's Spawn MC?" Bane asked.

Breaker shrugged as if it were no big deal. "I got too old. There comes a time in every man's life when whether he wants it or not, he simply gets too old. I was older than most of the guys in the MC when Deke took over. Finally, it was time. Deke and I left on good terms."

"Why are you here right now?" Bane demanded.

Breaker gazed at him for a minute then said, "I don't know who you are but that's between me and the MC."

"My name is Theo Franks and my niece and grandson are part of the MC. I'm here to look out for them."

Breaker looked over at Sarah. "And her? Is she your woman?"

Bane glanced over at Sarah and nodded. "I guess you could say that."

Sarah's eyes grew wide as she stared back at him. They had been together for almost a year now but only as friends. They hadn't taken that last step between friends to lovers yet.

"How much do you know about Bear's family?" Priest asked, breaking the silence in the room.

Breaker snorted. "I know his old man is finally out of prison, both the old man and his younger son. I also know both of them are coming here with plans to take the MC back." Shaking his head he said, "One of my buddies did time with Oscar and Oscar liked to run off a bit in the mouth. He was looking for his own guys while still inside. My friend told me he was there the day Oscar got out. He said there were four guys waiting for him outside the walls. He told me those guys were hard core badasses and most MC's wouldn't have them. At least not the ones he knew. Said they looked like Sons of Anarchy on steroids."

"And that is why you came back here isn't it?" Priest asked.

Breaker turned his head to glare at the other man. "Oscar and Matty Buckley are nothing but bad news. Bear was tough but Oscar is ten times worse. He went to jail thirty years ago on a murder charge and left his two boys on their own. The MC looked out for them as best they could but Bear just got wilder and wilder as he grew up. He was uncontrollable then and he got what he deserved in the end. It took Deke to show us that."

"What did the old man go to jail for?" Bane asked.

"He shot his wife when he caught her in bed with his best friend. When the truth came out in court it seems his wife didn't want the other man, he forced himself on her and she was trying to get away when Oscar came in." Breaker told them. "He got twenty years for that murder. The DA called it second degree murder with special circumstances, but old Oscar couldn't keep his nose clean inside the joint, he got extra years for a shanking inside. The guy wasn't dead, just left in a wheelchair for the rest of his life."

"And the brother?"

Breaker shrugged. "He served ten years for armed robbery and attempted murder. Following in daddy's footsteps all the way. Those two are very bad news and the men they're riding with are as bad if not worse than they are."

"How many men has Oscar picked up along the way?" Priest questioned.

"I've heard about a dozen or so." Breaker looked them both in the eyes.

"Deke can handle that many." Priest nodded.

Breaker shook his head. "I don't think you understand something here. These men don't give a shit about the law, they don't care about who they have to kill to get what they want either. From the rumors I've heard, they are working their way from Maine in no particular hurry and they are taking no prisoners. Right now, they're building a rep for themselves and it isn't a good one. They're looking forward to the bloodbath they hope to have once they get here. So far, they have four deaths to their belts and they plan on wiping the Sin's Bastards off the fuckin map. They will kill every man, woman and kid in that MC. Then take over the compound and businesses Deke and his boys have set up." He turned to Bane. "That will include your niece and grandson. They've had scouts come and go and the scouts have told them that Deke's got several businesses going and he's making good money. They plan on making even more by bringing the drug trade back to this area. And that's something Deke didn't want. He brought back a safe environment to not only the MC but this entire town. He looks out for the town's people here too and they have come to realize that, realize and appreciate it. If the MC falls under Oscar's rule, they won't have another safe day."

Bane's fingers turned to fists. "They won't get the chance. I won't let them anywhere near Cricket and Dusty."

Breaker shrugged. "They could be here in hours or days. War is coming to Troy and no one can stop it."

"Watch me," Bane vowed.

Chapter Two

An hour later Breaker was gone. Bane, Priest and Sarah were alone again. He'd told him all he knew about Oscar, Matty and Bear. Now the three of them needed to make plans.

Priest called Deke to set up a meeting. As much as Bane wanted to be present, he knew he couldn't be. He couldn't let himself be dragged back into his old life. That wasn't what he wanted. His do over would have been for nothing if anyone in the MC knew he was still alive. He just couldn't take the risk of anyone recognizing him. He might not look like the man he once was but his mannerisms were still the same and he couldn't risk it.

When Deke and his entourage showed up, Bane and Sarah stayed in the bedroom. The door was open so they could hear everything said, but they stayed out of sight.

Priest opened the door of his room to find more than just Deke on the other side. Stepping back, he noted the members of the MC were present and accounted for. Not only was Deke there, but so was Sam, Gator, Mountain, Iceman, Black Jack and several more that Priest didn't know by name. Then he saw Breaker return.

When Priest shut the door, he turned to face the solid wall of bikers.

"What the fuck is this all about?" Deke demanded as he crossed his big arms across his chest.

"I came here to warn you about a threat I can't ignore. A threat against your MC," Priest began.

"If you're talking about Bear's brother and dad we already know," Deke replied. "We're able to track them as they're making their way here and growing in numbers as they get closer to us."

Priest looked over at Breaker then back over at Deke. "Did he also tell you that Oscar's plan is to just shoot his way in? And that he'll shoot anybody wearing your colors? Man, woman or child?"

"Yeah he did," Deke admitted softly. With steel in his spine and in his words, he assured Priest, "We'll be ready for him."

"How can you be ready for that?" Priest scoffed. "I've been watching you for the last few days and you aren't ready for jack squat. Your women aren't sheltered nor are you on lock down." He shook his head.

Deke glared at him. "He isn't even close to us yet."

"You don't think so?" Priest asked softly. "If you think that then you'd be wrong. He's got at least three of his men scouting this town already. I've watched them watching your every move. They take note of who comes and goes from your compound. Don't tell me they aren't here yet."

"What else have you seen?" Sam demanded angrily.

"They've set up cameras on the businesses you guys own and operate and that includes Redemption House."

Deke didn't move but then he glanced over at his men and they all agreed, they hadn't seen anything either. He turned back to Priest. "How do you know all this?"

"My man James has been here a week now and he's very good at what he does. He notes everything and finds stuff that shouldn't be there but is."

"And how long have you been here?" Mountain asked.

Priest stared at the man. "Long enough."

The tension in the room just cranked up a notch and was turning hostile when Sarah stepped out of the bedroom and whispered loudly, "Please stop, all of you."

Everyone turned to see her standing there with tears running down her face.

"I can't bear this. You have to stop quarreling and fight together against what's coming. There is a battle coming that will require all of you to work together if you hope to win it."

"Who the fuck are you?" Sam growled as he scowled at her interruption.

"I'm no one that matters, but you guys..." She held out her hands toward them. "You guys matter, you guys, your women and families, they matter. Don't you dare ignore this or pass it off as nonsense. I may not know your world, but I know families matter and you need to do what you need to do to protect them." She put her fists on her hips and glared at each and every one of them. "This pissant has plans to take it all away from you if you allow it. He thinks he can surprise you and catch you with your pants down. He plans to wipe you out and he doesn't care who he has to hurt to get what he wants. You'd better not let him." With that, she turned and went back to the bedroom slamming the door behind her.

Deke looked around at the others in a dazed aura. "What the hell just happened?"

Sam snorted. "You just got your ass handed to you, fool."

Deke turned his head and viewed Priest for a moment. "Who was that woman?"

Priest shrugged. "To tell you the truth I have no clue who she is. She's a friend of a friend. But she's absolutely right. We are going to have to work together to live through this. You need to get ready. I can help you with that but you need to get your women and kids under protection."

"From what we can gather, Oscar and Matty and their ragtag group are still in Maine working their way south," Mountain stated.

Priest shook his head. "They're already in New Hampshire. They met up with several others in Concord. Word on the street is they're next stop is Lowell, Massachusetts. There is a group of survivalists waiting for them there." Shaking his head he informed them, "Four men who have no souls and think survival of the fittest is the key."

"And just how do you know that?" Mountain folded his massive arms over his chest.

"You have your ways and I have mine." Priest shrugged. He clocked Deke, "I've also heard when he picks up those four, he'll have enough men and will be coming here next."

Deke shook his head. "We need to know who he's got watching us right now then we'll take precautions. If we all go into high alerts this minute, his minions will tell him and then he'll come blasting into town. We have to protect everyone living in this town, not just us. That wouldn't be good for the town, wouldn't be good for us either."

The bedroom door opened, and Bane walked out and met the men standing there face to face. "Then you meet the fuckers head on and far away from this town and your families."

Deke straightened his spine and slowly turned to face the new man. He thought he recognized the voice but when he turned, he didn't know the man standing there. "Who the fuck are you?"

Bane shrugged. "I'm nobody."

"Why do I doubt that very much?" Deke snorted.

"I don't care what you think one way or the other," Bane retorted.

"What exactly are you saying?" Mountain asked.

Bane turned his head to the giant of a man standing there. "What I'm saying is that you need to take the fight to Oscar, rather than wait for him to bring the fight to you. Waiting is bad if you're the one doing it. Rattle his fucking cage if you like."

"Shock and awe, huh?" Sam, known as Bones nodded. "I like that. We could whittle down his numbers that way too. Take away his men, you take away his power in numbers."

Deke thought about what Bane was saying then nodded. "We also make the man desperate which in turn makes him careless. We have to let the club know what's going on before we come up with a plan of action."

Bane nodded. "Do it now before you lose the element of surprise, because once that is gone he'll come straight through the heart of your club. He wants to bring devastation to this town and he isn't going to stop until either you or he is dead. Remember, he's had seventeen years to plan his revenge and prison changes a man. And it's never for the good."

"Huh…" Mountain grumbled. "From what I've heard of Oscar Buckley, prison only enhanced his ugliness."

Priest nodded. "I've heard the same thing. His history reveals he was an ugly, mean bastard before he went inside. His murder charge told us that much. I read his files from prison and he wasn't a model citizen. From day one, he pushed and pushed. So by the time he ended his first year, he ran his prison block. He ran everything from drugs to cigarettes inside. The other prisoners called him *Jefe*."

Deke scoffed, "I really don't care what they called him. He's a dead man walking as far as I'm concerned."

Sam looked over at Priest. "Do we know where they are right now?"

Priest shrugged. "Somewhere near Concord, New Hampshire was the last word I got."

"Is there any way to verify that?" Deke questioned.

Priest turned and walked out to the door across the hall and knocked on James's door. He spoke to the other man for a moment then returned. Leaving the door open, he waited until James joined them.

He looked up at the group of men facing him and informed them, "When we first heard about this threat we were able to track them down. We put trackers on their bikes and have been following them on their journey. The trackers have told us every stop they've made so far."

Mountain and Sam looked around making eye contact with the others before they turned back to James and Priest.

"How the fuck did you do all that?" Sam asked.

Priest just looked at him. "We have our ways."

"How did you find them in the first place?" Wiley wanted to know.

"They never tried to hide who they were and what they were doing," James admitted. "It was rather easy to find them and tag them. They were building their army to confront you."

Breaker nodded. "They got a few original members on their team. The ones who were here under Bear. You threw them out when they wouldn't agree to your terms." He shrugged and added, "The only real thing you changed was the drug dealing. You didn't want it but they liked the money it brought to the club. Even paying Bear his forty percent was bringing them more money than they ever had before. They figure they have a score to settle with you for changing their lives. They liked the way Bear ran things, but you turned the MC around and went legit. They missed the money they got from the drug sales you wouldn't let them deal."

Deke shook his head. "I gave them a chance and a choice. I never wanted to boot anyone out of their home, but I didn't want the MC to keep going down a dead-end one-way path either. I wanted to build it up and set us on a different path than the one Bear had it on. If we'd have kept going on his path, everyone would have been dead or in jail within three to five years' time."

Breaker nodded. "We all knew that. We hated it, but no one had the balls to stand up to Bear until you came around. You showed us a different way. Bear just took what he wanted, you gave us a choice. Bear just took and took, you honored your word."

Deke turned and glared at Bane. "Which leaves us with you...who are you and what is your interest in all of this?" He glanced over at Priest and nodded. "I get why he's here, why are you?"

Before Bane walked out to confront these men he'd made up his mind that he would tell them as close to the truth as possible without telling them everything. "I have my reasons. But I will tell you this much, I don't like the fact Oscar Buckley thinks he can just walk over good men to get his MC back. You guys have a good thing going here and you take care of your families. That shows you have honor and believe me when I say, that's rare in today's world."

"So what's in this for you?" Sam queried. "You don't seem the type to do this out of the goodness of your heart."

Bane shrugged. "I don't really give a fuck what you think, nor do I have to explain why I'm here. Right now, you need all the help you can get. All you have to know about me is the fact I'm here, willing to help you."

Deke snapped his head around to glare at Bane. "If I find you betrayed us I'll personally put a bullet in your head. Just saying..."

Bane nodded. "I'll give you a gun if it comes to that."

"Is the woman yours or his?" Sam nodded at Priest.

"She's mine," Bane assured him. "She isn't your concern either."

Sam shook his head. "Never said she was, just pairing up who's with who, that's all. She's your responsibility."

"Damn right she is." Bane growled. "You just remember that."

Sam nodded. "No problem. My own woman is waiting for me at home."

"Can we get back to the main issue here?" Deke grumbled.

James stepped forward and handed him three different photos. "These are the men watching your businesses. Facial recognition hasn't identified them yet, but I'm working on that."

"Have you checked with Trudy yet?" Mountain asked.

James nodded. "I passed them to her yesterday but she hasn't come up with anything yet either. Either these guys are clean or they've never been caught before."

"There has to be some kind of record on these guys," Deke added.

James nodded. "If there is anything out there we'll find it, don't worry. Between Trudy and myself we can find anything."

Deke glared at the man. "Trudy, I know. I don't know you. Don't give me your word when you might not be able to back it up."

James nodded once to let him know he got the message.

"What I suggest you do is gather your members and your families and get them under your protection for now," Priest interjected. "Keep them close. Then a small select group can go hunt down the men waiting for Buckley in Lowell. Maybe some of the men from the original MC don't know."

"Then what? My men aren't killers. This would be cold-blooded murder. You're suggesting we take them out before they can take us out." Deke growled.

"Sometimes life gives you a choice," Bane commented. "You have to choose this time between life and death for you and your families. This is a no-win situation. It's kill or be killed."

Deke gritted his teeth. "Yes, we belong to an MC but we aren't cold blooded killers. We'll fight if we're attacked first but this isn't that yet, is it? I can't ask my men to kill before they storm our gates. I just can't."

It was at that moment Bane knew what he had to do. He looked over at Priest and saw the only answer they had in his eyes as well. Looking over at James, he saw the solution there as well. He gave them both a nod and from that, a pact was born. The three of them would take on the MC formed from Buckley's hate of Deke.

He turned back to Deke. "You take care of your families here. Don't you dare lose *any* one of them." Then he turned and walked back into the bedroom slamming the door behind him. He looked over at Sarah but didn't say anything. Bane knew he was being sucked back into his past and he didn't like it. It wasn't that he couldn't do it, he could kill without remorse and had done so in the past but he was trying to start a new life now. He hated the fact he was drawn back but he couldn't allow this to happen. These people needed his help. He couldn't undo the past but he could do this. His blood began to rush through his body and for the first time in a long time, he felt good. His past had been all about taking life, maybe his thinking that was truly his path had been all wrong. Here he was still taking lives but the reason behind it was ultimately to save lives. Maybe this would begin to heal his soul.

Chapter Three

Bane went over to the window and looked out over the city. He felt more than saw Sarah move in behind him. Then her arms came around his waist and she pressed her body into his back. "What's going on?" she whispered. Maybe she shouldn't be touching him but she was risking it. She wanted him to know she was willing to stick by him always.

"My past is catching up with me and I don't like it." He glared out the window.

Sarah swallowed hard, but fear wouldn't let her say anything. She'd always known this man had a past, maybe even a violent past, everyone did but she didn't ask about it because if she didn't know about it, his past couldn't hurt her. She hated her own past... hated what she'd done and was ashamed of it.

For a moment, her own eyes were haunted. She hadn't wanted to come back to this part of the state. It was too close to the town she'd grown up in, too close to *his* family. Because of *him,* she hadn't seen her own mother for the last five years. She had had to break all ties to her brother as well and that really hurt her. She and Stone had been very close at one point. But Stone had always been a stickler for the truth and she knew he'd found out about her lies. She didn't think he would forgive her for all the lies she and her mother told him over the years.

The lies had been told to keep him focused on the delicate job he was doing in the battlefields. They didn't want him to be distracted and maybe end up bleeding or dead on those same battlefields. They kept the truth from him and she knew he couldn't overlook what she'd done. Resting her forehead on Bane's back, she breathed in his scent.

She could smell laundry soap and citrus and she felt her mouth water. Drawing in a deep breath, of it as his own unique scent was a mixture of spicy and sweet. Sarah almost groaned as she felt her body's response to him. She'd been hiding what she felt for Bane for a while now and she was almost out of patience. She wanted him badly, but she also knew he didn't want her the same way.

"Sarah," he said. "What are you doing?"

"Nothing," she whispered. "I'm not doing anything." She broke her hold and stepped away from him reluctantly.

~*~

Bane turned slowly to face her. What he saw was Sarah's head hung low, her face covered by her long dark hair, but he could also see her trembling as she took another tiny step away from him.

He reached out and cupped her chin bringing her face up to meet his. He saw the longing in her eyes before she could hide it and for the first time he understood what she wanted. Sarah wanted him! His hand shook as he rubbed his thumbs over her cheeks. Somehow, his heart began to beat a little quicker in his body. It beat so hard he could feel it thunder in his chest. "Shall we get our own room?" he whispered.

Sarah was so lost in his eyes she couldn't speak so she nodded.

He reached out and grabbed her hand.

Leaving the bedroom, Bane noted the room was empty save for Priest and James. He glanced over their way. "We're going to get a room and get settled in. I'll be back later."

Priest nodded and barely looked at him as he and James continued to make plans for the upcoming battle.

Bane didn't pause but continued on his way to the front desk. When he got the room, he hauled her up three flights and opened the door to the suite. Then he pulled her in and slammed the door shut. Twisting the lock, he pushed her against the portal and lifted her face so he could see her eyes.

"I need to know something," he spoke in a hushed voice.

"What?" she whispered back, licking her dry lips with her tongue as her eyes connected with his.

Bane was distracted for a moment by the movement of her tongue and he groaned slightly. His body temperature rose as he asked, "Do you want me?" He didn't understand the rush going through him at the moment. He'd never felt this before, not even with his Grace. With Grace, he desired her, he enjoyed taking her body, but she didn't look at him the same way Sarah did. He'd been feeling this rush for a while now but he would never cross that line with her if she didn't want him to. But this, this would change their relationship and he had to know if she wanted that.

Sarah closed her eyes briefly but when she felt his hand wrap around her throat she opened them again. The look in his eyes told her he was as hungry for her as she was for him. "Yes, I want you," she whispered. "I think I've wanted you for a long time, maybe my whole life."

Bane paused for a moment then spoke, "I'm not an easy man to get along with. I don't do the whole love thing, never have and I don't know if I ever could. I didn't know what real life was all about before I found you. I was married once but that didn't work out. I thought I wanted her but I couldn't keep her." He looked into her eyes and was honest with her. "I didn't know what it was like for her until I lost her. I never felt like this with her and I thought I was in love with her or at least I thought I cared about her. But she never loved me back."

"Maybe you just haven't had the right woman before." She gazed into his eyes. "I could be that woman for you if you'd let me."

Bane leaned toward her. "I have to know something."

"What's that?" she whispered as he got even closer.

"If we do this, you will belong to me. Is that what you want? I'm a possessive man and I don't share what's mine." He paused and knew she got his message when her hand rose to the side of his bearded jaw.

Bane leaned in the last inch or so then his mouth crashed down on hers and that was all she wrote. Sparks blew as their lips came together and both felt the burn left in its wake. Bane groaned and Sarah gasped.

He thrust his tongue down her throat and lust rushed through both of them.

His fingers tore her clothing off and threw them to the floor. Within minutes, she was standing in front of him naked and he drank in her view. Every curve was under his review and he groaned. "You're beautiful." He croaked.

The only thing she wore was a golden chain around her neck with a single gem dangling on the fragile thread. The stone was set in an old fashioned setting but was indeed very unique. He meant to ask about it but right now, he had other things on his mind.

She moaned and tried to hide her old life. He might not see her scars just yet but she knew they were there. "I need to see you too," she reminded him shyly.

Bane stepped away and tore his own clothes off. Usually, he was rather picky about his clothing but that wasn't the case today. Today, he didn't care. He'd never felt this kind of rush before, not even with Grace and to him she was the one he thought would be his forever. Now, here today, he just wanted inside this woman. Never had he felt this intenseness, this rush. He grabbed her up into his arms and stalked her over to the bed. Throwing her down, he followed her and opened her legs to his view.

"Tell me to go or stay but if I stay, there will be no one else. This body will be mine. It will belong to me and me alone. I'm the kind of man who doesn't share."

Sarah looked deep into his eyes, "Take me. I need you and you alone."

"I can't be gentle this time. I need you and this too much."

"It's okay," she assured him as she cupped his face with her hand. "I've wanted you for many months. I want you any way I can get."

Bane thrust into her core and immediately felt her wrap around his cock. She was wet and warm and he felt a moment of resistance. His eyes widened as he realized why. His eyes snapped to hers and he saw her flinch in pain. "What the hell?" he gasped as he tried to pull out.

She wrapped her legs around his waist and wouldn't let him go. "I need you. Please don't stop."

Bane paused briefly then pulled out enough to thrust back inside her, then he lost control and nothing would stop him at that point. His strokes got harder and faster than he ever thought he could do before her.

Neither of them could stop the rush of excitement barreling toward them. Sarah fell apart in his arms. She gasped then cried out as she crossed over the threshold of ecstasy.

Bane felt her explode and three thrusts later, he flew over the edge. He couldn't stop it as it was almost like he had no resistance to her needs. Calling out her name, he smothered her lips with his as he emptied himself deep inside her. He laid his forehead on hers and his breathing was harsh for a moment or two. Then he lifted his weight off her and slid down at her side. Cupping her chin, he turned her to face him.

Sarah reluctantly opened her eyes to face the music.

"How are you still a virgin?" he asked quietly.

Sarah looked at him and boldly told him, "I'm twenty-nine years old and I'm not ashamed of the fact that I waited. I wanted to feel something for the man I gave my innocence to. I'm glad it was you. You're the first man I ever felt anything except fear for."

"You know I'm too old for you right?" he informed her. "My kids were older than you are right now."

Sarah's body jerked. "Your kids?" she squeaked. She had heard him talk about his kids but she had no idea they were still alive. He'd always talked about them in the past.

"I had two kids, a son and a daughter but that was in my old life. A life I no longer want. I don't think I could live that life anymore. I've been away from it for a year now and you know something? I don't really even miss it."

"And where are they now?"

"They both died a while back," Bane admitted.

Sarah studied him for a moment then noticed the hardness in him for the first time. She trembled in fear of him for the first time. "I don't know the real you do I?" she finally whispered.

Bane shook his head. "No, you don't. I thought I could start my life over as a new man, a different man but I can't."

"Yes, you can." Raising her hand to his face she whispered, "You are a strong man. A vibrant man, you can leave the past in the past and move on with your new life if that's really what you want."

Bane raised his eyes to hers. He plucked her hand off his cheek and kissed her fingertips. "My dear woman, you don't know who I was in my past. That would be impossible."

~*~

Sarah closed her eyes as tears squeezed through her eyelids. "We all have secrets. We all have a past we wish never happened."

Bane studied her for a moment then had to ask, "What could a woman as sweet as you ever do to cause this much sadness?"

Sarah stared into his eyes and didn't speak for a moment. She didn't know if she could even tell him about her past. She had lived with this for twelve years now and only one other person knew what really happened that night. She'd been alone and living in fear since then and now, she was tired of living this way. Maybe Bane couldn't help her but at least with him she felt strong enough to take the chance. She swallowed hard and then she whispered her sins to him, "I killed a man."

Bane looked shocked at her confession. He didn't speak for a moment then he shook his head. "That can't be true. You could never hurt anyone."

Sarah's tears rolled down her face. "But it's true. I did kill him and I would do it again. Jack Connors deserved to die and I don't regret a moment what I did to him."

"What happened?"

Sarah moved away from him or at least she tried but Bane wasn't going to let her. He brought her back to his side and he waited for her to speak.

Sarah swallowed hard and tried to gather her thoughts. "My mom was widowed when I was a baby. She got married again a year later and she picked the worst man but it really wasn't her fault. He hid his bad side until he couldn't hide it any more. He never really liked my brother and me. He ran my brother off when he was eighteen. He made it impossible for him to stay in that house. I was a lot younger than Stone, so I was stuck living with him and mom. I got to see the real Jack in a way my brother never could. You see, Jack liked to drink a lot and when he drank, he got mean and nasty. Mom always sent me to my room and told me to lock the door when he began drinking. She tried to keep me safe and that worked for a while but pretty soon a locked door wouldn't keep him out." She paused and swallowed hard. Fresh tears rolled down her cheeks. "When I was fourteen he tried to rape me. My mom stopped him but she took a beating for interfering. He hurt her so bad I vowed that it would never happen again."

"What happened?"

"When I was fifteen he began drinking and staring at me. When he got up to get another beer, Mom knew what was about to happen and she sent me to my room. She told me to lock the door. She told me not to come out no matter what I heard."

"What did you hear?"

"When Jack came back, he noticed I was gone and he blew a gasket. They began yelling and screaming at each other. It got real bad really fast. I heard my mom screaming and I knew he was hurting her and I couldn't stand it. I came out of my room with my baseball bat in my hand. He was strangling her and I swung my bat. He hit the floor with a thud but he let her go and I kept hitting him again and again. It was like all the rage and fear I lived with over the years was right there and I just couldn't stop." She shuddered as the memories came rushing back. "There was so much blood, it was scary." Her voice had dropped to a bare whisper and she looked at him. "Mom tried to stop me but I couldn't. It wasn't until she wrapped her arms around me that I stopped. Jack was dead and I was so scared. Jack Connors had three brothers and a father that never liked me. Hell, they could barely handle being around my mom but me? If they knew I killed Jack, they would have killed me on sight. After the funeral, I had to leave. I wouldn't put anything past those bastards, so Mom and I left town. I didn't trust leaving mom behind. They blamed her for his death and they were coming to settle the score. I got my mom settled in another town under a different name and then I left. I couldn't risk staying around her and bringing Jack's family to her door. I changed my name and never looked back. I've been running for fourteen years now."

Bane felt a rage rushing through his body. Not for her but for the men who caused this tragedy in her life. "You left home at fifteen?"

Sarah nodded. "I had to, don't you see? I had to protect my mother."

"Have you seen her since?"

"Once or twice. From a distance. But Jack's brothers and father are still looking for me, so I can't go back for her yet."

"What about your brother? Stone, I think you called him."

Sarah nodded. "I haven't seen him in so long." She trailed off at the end of her statement. "I don't even know if he wants to see me. You see, I lied to him many years ago. I told him there was nothing wrong at home. I led him to believe mom and I were safe. Stone isn't one to forgive lies and deception. He always told me growing up to tell the truth. He was so much older than I was that I looked up to him. I promised never to lie to him and I did. I lied to him."

"I think he would understand," Bane assured her.

She shook her head. "You don't know my brother. He can be a stubborn ass when he wants to be."

"I think he'd be more concerned about you than worrying about the lie you told. He must be looking for you."

Sarah shrugged. "I don't know if he is or not. I had to break all my ties in order to hide from Jack's brothers. I changed my name a few times over the years and I kept running. It seems like I've been running my whole life. I'm afraid if I stay in one place too long, they'll find me."

"Maybe once we settle things here you should reach out to your brother. Maybe if you can find him and tell him the truth he could forgive you for the past."

Sarah felt the tears roll down her cheeks. "I wouldn't know where to start looking for him."

"Maybe you could ask James." Bane smiled. "He claims he can find anything."

"Maybe," she gulped. Hesitating, she whispered, "But what if he doesn't want anything to do with me and my lies?"

"Then he'd be a fool," Bane assured her.

Sarah rested her forehead on his chest. She dared to have hope in her heart for reaching out to her brother but she knew she couldn't drag him into this situation with Jack's brothers. "I can't reach out yet. I won't bring this down on his shoulders. This is my mess not his."

"Honey, you've been running for all these years, you have to stop and face your past. I know that's hard and you may not want to do it but that's the only way you can be safe."

"I don't know if I can," she whispered brokenly.

Chapter Four

Bane joined Priest and James in Priest's room. He'd left Sarah sleeping after another go round with him. He felt energized by what they shared but she was worn out. He paused for a moment to allow these feelings to wash over him. The sex he just had…it'd been nothing like before in his life. He actually *felt* things with this woman. It had been as if he was the virgin. A newbie to the world of feeling and emotions.

He knocked on the door.

Priest opened it and motioned him inside.

James had pages laid out on the coffee table and Bane moved over there to see what they had. They were prison records that showed the men and their mug shots along with a list of the crimes they'd gone to jail for. None of the men he found there were saints, in fact each and every one of them looked as if killing wouldn't bother them at all.

Bane looked over at Priest. "This is Oscar's crew?"

Priest nodded. "Each of them were handpicked by Oscar and Matty."

"So how do we stop them?"

Priest turned to stare at him. Then he asked a very important question, "How bloody are you willing to get on this mission?"

Bane glared at the other man before he said, "As bloody as it takes to stop the war. Oscar and Matty Buckley will never get here."

Priest nodded. "We'll stay as much in the background as we can but we may not always be able to stay in the shadows." He paused. "We're going to have to put these men down, you realize that. We can't allow them to regroup or finish what Oscar has started."

Bane nodded. "I know and I'm ready." He shuddered then stood taller. "What's our first step?"

"I think we should find the survivalists and neutralize them before Oscar and the rest of his group even gets to Lowell," Priest informed him.

Bane felt this was smart as he nodded then turned to James. "When this is over I need you to find someone for me."

"Oh, who might that be?"

"Sarah's brother, Stone. I also need some information on Jack Connors and his family."

"Who is Jack Connors?" Priest frowned.

"Jack is Sarah's stepfather. Something bad happened to Jack a lifetime ago and I need to know what I'm up against with her." He stared at both men. "I just want to know the players, that's all. I have no plans to kill them if that's what you think."

Priest nodded. "Ok, but whatever you find you share with us and we can all decide what to do about it."

"Ok, what do you have in mind for the men in Lowell?"

"Other than neutralizing them?" Priest shrugged. "I really hadn't planned that far yet. Why, what did you have in mind?"

"Circle of life my friend." Bane smiled as if he had a huge secret in mind. "Something I noticed the last time I was here." Then he went on to suggest what he had in mind.

When he was finished, Priest pulled him aside and after a moment, he told the other man, "James and I can do this on our own, if you like. I know you wanted a new life for yourself and if you do this, you won't ever make a clean break from it. All of this…" He motioned at the new face and all the pain Bane had endured over the last year. "All of this will have been for nothing."

Bane thought for a moment then nodded. "A year ago, I might have changed my mind. Hell, I might not have done it at all. But I saw something today, something that told me I have to be here. I had to help that MC."

"Oh, what was that?" Priest looked curious.

Bane grinned. "I saw Cricket. She was walking down the street pushing a baby stroller, and inside that stroller were three babies. They weren't newborn babies but they weren't that old either. A year ago, she would have been pregnant with them when I saw her last. She would have been far enough along that she knew they were growing inside her already. You weren't here a year ago, so you wouldn't have seen her stand up to me then. As you know, the MC was willing to go to war with Zevon Stark to protect her and she was willing to die to protect them. Stark had put a contract out on her life and when she found out about it she begged me for three days. She wanted three days before I killed her, just to say goodbye to her life."

"You would have killed her?" Priest crossed his arms over his chest and glared at him.

Bane shook his head. "No, I wasn't here to kill her. I only brought the message of the contract. Then three men from Stark's camp found her. They would have killed her and not for the money either. They would have killed her because they were afraid of Stark."

"What's your point?"

"My point is Cricket didn't whine about the possibility there was a hit out on her, she didn't hide behind the MC and she didn't run. She showed more fucking courage by facing her demise than I'd ever seen before." He paused, then looked at Priest. "In this line of work you and I have met some powerful men, men who think money rules the world, men who think everyone has their price. Cricket's never had anything and yet she stood her ground. She lived those three days like she had nothing left to lose. She even married her man the second day. The men who'd hired me over the years would have tried bribery, threats and they would have pissed their pants at the sight of a barrel of a gun shoved in their slimy faces. They would have thrown their families under the bus to get away if they had to. Cricket didn't do that. You want to know something else? The contract should have been on my daughter Cordelia, not Cricket. Cordelia was the one who did the deed in the first place, Cordelia is the one who betrayed Stark not Cricket. But Stark didn't care, he wanted blood and would not be denied. When the MC wanted to ride against Stark, she wouldn't let them. That little girl wouldn't put anyone in her place. That took a great deal of courage and an almost forgotten sense of honor. I've only seen that sense of honor from one man before and she never knew that man. That man was my grandfather. He may have been a killer like me but he had that sense of honor. He tried to teach it to me but my feelings were never like his. I could kill without remorse but when she did that, I remembered that old man."

Priest listened and held no emotion on his face.

"No one in my life ever did anything like that for me. No one ever stood up for me either, but she did that for her family. And she considered the MC her family." He shook his head. "Yes, I could take the easy way out and not put myself out there for them but that wouldn't do. This situation might drag me back into my old life, kicking and screaming but I'm doing this for her. I'm doing it for my grandfather as well."

Priest stared at him for a moment then nodded. "Are you going to tell her you're still alive?"

Bane shook his head. "No, I don't think so. I thought about it, I really did, but no. I let the Jessin name die out a year ago when I was bleeding out after the battle with Stark. She took who she thought was me home and buried me when I expected her to spit on my grave. But I can't walk away from her either, so whether she wants it or not I'm her fucking guardian angel. Hell, whether I want it or not, I *am* her guardian angel."

Priest smiled faintly. "I know how that feels too. My Sawyer and the Hell's Fire Riders got me too. I can't change that and neither can they. My wife and son keep me grounded and the Hell's Fire Riders give me purpose. They are my second chance, my do over."

"The question is what do I do after this, always supposing we survive?" Bane asked.

"One thing at a time old man, one thing at a time." Priest grinned as he slapped the other man on the shoulder and they both turned back to the table and James's information.

They quickly finalized the arrangements and set their course.

Priest made a phone call to Deke, while Bane went back to his own room to tell Sarah what they were going to do.

He closed the door behind him and walked quietly over to the bed where Sarah was laying. Her eyes were open and she watched him approach without saying a word. He stood over her for a moment then held out his hand. She paused for a moment then reached out and wrapped her fingers with his.

Bane sat down on the edge of the bed and still looking at her he whispered, "I don't know why you came to me and I don't know why you stayed all this time. As I said before, I'm not an easy man to get to know, but I do know I would miss you if you left. I have this mission coming up shortly and I need to know if you'll be here when I return."

Sarah closed her eyes then brought her hand and his closer to her chest. Splaying out his fingers against her chest, she allowed him to feel the beat of her heart. "My heart beats for you and you alone. You may not want it but it does. I know you've lived your whole life thinking you don't have feelings but I don't believe that. You and I wouldn't be here if that were true. You may feel differently than everyone else but you do have them."

Bane couldn't speak, as his throat grew thick.

"Yes I'll be here," she vowed. "I'll wait forever for you to return if I have to." She reached up with her free hand and laid it against his jaw and whispered, "Please come home to me. I need you. I need you to come back to me."

Bane nodded. "We're leaving in a few minutes to try and stop the threat. I don't know when we'll be back but sweetheart, I will come back to you. Now that I know the sweet taste of you, I will be back."

Sarah nodded, then she sat up in bed as her hands went to the back of her neck and she unclasped her necklace. She pooled the necklace in the base of his hand and told him, "My mother gave this to me the last time I saw her. She'd always worn it from the first time I could remember. She used to tell me it was her talisman against the evil of the world. This necklace has been passed down from generation to generation. My great grandfather gave it to his wife well over a hundred years ago. I don't know if it really works or not but I want you to take it with you. If there is magic in the stone I want it to watch over you on this mission."

Bane closed his hand over the necklace and swallowed hard. "Thank you." He didn't know what else to say, no one had ever cared if he lived or died before this.

Sarah closed her eyes and whispered brokenly, "P-please come back to me. You mean a great deal to me and I want more time with you."

"As do I with you," he assured her.

A knock sounded on the door and Bane got up to react to the summons.

~*~

In a little less than three hours, they arrived in Lowell, Massachusetts. Darkness was just falling and the shadows would hide them while they did their jobs. Locating the survivalists wasn't as hard as they thought. James had done his homework and had worked out where the men were waiting.

They found them in a shack on the edge of town. The men were not concerned about anyone finding them and that was always a bad sign. Priest had determined that they couldn't just blow up the place which in a way disappointed Bane. He explained that they had to take them out one at a time and in a hurry. These men were the last piece of Buckley's plan for the destruction of the Sin's MC.

Priest reasoned that if they took them out one by one whoever was the last one would think the others had changed their mind and backed out of the deal. It made sense, but they had little time to make that happen. Maybe only hours which meant they had to move now. It also set up the possibility that the last person alive could contact Buckley and tell him about the others.

Priest and Bane waited in the shadows as James moved toward their bikes. He added a little something to each bike and then without warning came back to where they were waiting.

"What did you do?" Bane asked.

James glared at him. "I put sugar in their gas tanks. That will seize up their engines and then we can pick them off one at a time."

"We don't have time for all of that," Bane grumbled. "Buckley could be here anytime."

Priest glared at him. "We don't have much of a choice here. If we take them all out at once, Buckley will know someone is trying to stop them and he'll be more determined to stop us. Right now, he has the upper hand or so he thinks."

"Ok, so how does this work then?" Bane asked with impatience.

"We draw them out, get them to chase us and then we kill them and hide their bodies."

Bane looked back at the shack and the bikes in front of it. Studying the sight in front of him, he noted the fact that the bikes sitting there looked almost new. Turning to the two men, he grinned. "Let's find out just how brave these bastards think they are."

"What do you have in mind?" Priest asked him.

Bane leaned in and told him of his plan.

Priest and James listened carefully and then all three agreed on his plan.

Priest disappeared in the shadows, then James and finally Bane disappeared into the darkness.

A few moments later, the silence of the night was shattered by the sound of a single bullet hitting the gas tank of one the four bikes sitting in front of the shack. The explosion rocked the area and the bike blew apart.

Four men rushed the front door. Each of them had a small handgun and each of them rushed in a different direction. A shot rang out and the first man went down. The other three looked around to see if they could find the person shooting at them. Of course, they couldn't see him, he was hidden in the trees.

Another shot rang out and the second man went down. The other two took up a defensive position and again, searched for the shooter. They looked in every direction as the second shot came from a different direction than the first.

When the third shot took out the third man, the remaining man looked ready to piss his pants. He gazed around in all four directions.

The three men standing there watching him could almost see the man coming apart. Sweat matted the man's hair to his head. His eyes were wild as he searched in front of him then the man turned and he searched behind him, then to his left and his right. "Who the fuck is out there and what the fuck do you want?" the man shouted out.

"We want you, motherfucker," James shouted out.

"Why?" the man asked as he swiped his hand over his mouth. "I didn't do anything to you."

"But you did, asshole," Priest yelled back. "You were willing to join a man in his quest to slaughter innocent people. You know who I'm talking about!"

The fourth man paused and nodded as he muttered something none of them could hear. When he went to reach in his pocket, Bane put a bullet through his hand. The man screamed and his other hand went to cover the hole in his wrist.

"Throw your gun away then stand up," Priest ordered his target.

"What? So you can shoot me in the head? I don't think so." He looked around again. "I'll just keep my gun if you don't mind. I got all night. You are the ones who hide in the shadows."

"You think Buckley will allow you to live when he gets here?" Priest laughed at him. "He'll put a bullet in your head when he hears how you betrayed him."

"But I haven't betrayed anyone!" the other man screamed.

"Buckley won't believe that," James shouted. "He'll think you gave us information to save your own slimy hide."

"But I didn't," the man yelled out. "I haven't told you nothing!"

"He won't believe that for a moment. He'll kill you just for surviving. When he sees the other three are gone, he will not understand at all," Priest stated real facts. "If you think for one moment, he'll let you live, you're only kidding yourself. You'll be useless to him now. He wanted all four of you."

"You lousy bastards. You killed all four of us, even if you leave me alive I'm still a dead man!" The man knelt in the dirt. He was holding his pistol against his forehead while contemplating his options.

Without warning, another shot rang out and the man hiding fell into the dirt. He was screaming in pain, holding his side.

Bane saw Priest walking out of the shadows.

The man noticed him and brought his bloody hand up. His weapon was shaking as he held it on Priest.

Priest paused and told him, "You won't live long enough to pull the trigger, should you choose to. You have two more guns on you and they both have their hands on the trigger."

"What...what the fuck do you want from me?" the man asked as he blood poured from his wound.

"Was your life worth getting mixed up with a man like Oscar Buckley?" Priest asked as he stood over the other man's bleeding body.

"I had nothing before this came up, no wife or sweetheart so I figured I had nothing to lose and who knows, I might have survived long enough to enjoy what he promised."

"And what did he promise you?"

The man swallowed hard, blood began to drain out of the corner of his mouth. His eyes were glazing over and his skin was turning grey. "Oscar promised us a place of our own. A place at his table and a roof over our heads. That's what he promised us."

"What did he expect you to do for all of that?"

"He wanted us to find a secret way in. He said someone was working with him and all we had to do was locate a tunnel from the compound to the woods behind the fence line." The man's words trailed off and his words were nothing more than a whisper as he took his last breath. Then there was nothing. He died staring at the night sky.

Priest turned and narrowed his eyes at where Bane was standing.

A few minutes later, Bane and James joined him and Priest glared at both men. "There's a traitor in the compound. Someone who knows a way in and out of the compound. One that I doubt Deke knows about."

Bane turned and regarded the shack the men had been in a few minutes ago. He took one step toward it then another and another. He felt the Priest behind him and that was fine with him. Pushing the door open, he saw the gear the survivalists had waiting.

There were full backpacks with climbing gear and ropes, shovels and pickaxes. On the table was paperwork and maps. Bane looked over the maps carefully and soon found a pattern and something familiar. His heart grew cold as he studied the area on the map.

Gathering up the information, they found he nodded at Priest. "We have to get back while there's still time."

"Time for what?" Priest frowned.

"Time to set a trap to catch Buckley before he gets inside the clubhouse," Bane assured him. Looking around, he didn't see James. "Where is your buddy?"

"James is taking care of the bodies. He's pulling them deeper into the woods for the local wolf population to feast on." He looked around at the dump.

"What are you going to do with the bikes?" Bane asked.

"We've already pulled the blown up one away. The rest I think we should leave here. If Buckley and his men use them they won't get very far."

Bane nodded. "But then they would know someone is waiting for them and we could lose the element of surprise."

Priest shrugged. "We'd lose that element anyway at some point."

"True enough," Bane agreed. "But we have to get back to the compound right now. There is a secret way in that Deke may or may not know about. Now only the upper echelon of the old MC might know of this secret way in and out so that makes me think there could be a traitor working on the inside. I don't know if it's one of the men Buckley has with him or—"

"It could be Breaker." Priest followed his train of thought. "Maybe he came back not to stand with Deke against Buckley but instead to open up the tunnel leading into the compound *for* Buckley."

Priest shook his head. "Damn that man, doesn't he realize that once he's inside, Buckley will have a bullet with his name on it?"

"Did your man James find out anything on Breaker?" Bane asked. "Maybe something that Buckley could use against him?"

"We didn't look that far into him as he said he was working with Deke not against him," Priest admitted.

"Well, maybe you should dig a little deeper," Bane suggested. "Whether the traitor is in the group Buckley is riding with or it's Breaker himself, we need to know."

"I know he'll start looking when we leave here and by the time we get back to Troy, he should have some answers."

"What about this Trudy person?" Bane asked. "Could she get the information we need faster?" Bane asked.

"Maybe I can ask her." Priest nodded.

"We need to give Deke a head's up on this. Find out if he knows about the tunnel or not."

Priest nodded. "And if he doesn't have a clue that the tunnel exists? What then?"

"Then we get his attention and let him know he could have a traitor in his midst. He needs to know who he can trust from the men around him." Bane sighed. He knew this wouldn't be pleasant. Deke's men had been with him for years.

Chapter Five

James returned and they left the shack. They decided to leave the bikes behind after dragging the blown up one deep into the woods. If anyone tried to ride the bikes, they wouldn't get very far.

Bane took all the paperwork he found on the table with him to show to Deke. While Priest drove back, James was on the phone to Trudy to begin getting background on Breaker and the members of the old MC who had left when Deke didn't want to keep drugs on the menu.

They had to find the traitor and find out what Oscar had in mind. If Deke made the mistake of placing the women and children in the basement and Oscar got to them before Deke realized what was going on, that would be like handing them over for slaughter. That scenario was unacceptable.

A few hours later when they arrived in Troy, Deke, Sam, Black Jack and Mountain were waiting for them at their hotel. Priest opened the door to his room and all seven men walked in.

Deke walked over to the window and looked out over the city, then he turned back to confront Priest. "You'd better have a good explanation as to what's going on here," he growled. "You call me out of the blue and tell me I may have a traitor within my ranks. I trust each and every one of my men and you come out of the blue and tell me one of them is working with Buckley. How the fuck did you figure that out?"

Priest glared at the men in front of him. "We found a map of an underground tunnel that leads straight from outside the fence to the basement of the clubhouse. I didn't know if you knew about it or not, but Buckley knows about it."

Deke stared at him then looked over at his men. None of them looked as if they knew about this tunnel either. "How the fuck did you find this information?"

James stepped over to the table and began spreading out the documents they found at the shack out on the table.

Deke, Sam, Black Jack and Mountain stepped forward and began studying the documents.

Deke raised his head and glared at Priest. "I've never seen these drawings before. There were fifteen members of the old MC that stayed with us. Over the years, we've lost ten, either by death or the fact they wanted something they couldn't get with the new MC. We still have five members that have been there longer than me."

"You can't forget about Breaker," Bane reminded them.

Deke snapped his head and glared at Bane. "Breaker saved my life seventeen years ago. I doubt he's setting us up now. He chose to stay with us and helped me rebuild the MC the way it is today." Shaking his head he said, "I can't see him turning on us now."

James glanced down at his incoming text. Frowning, he read the message Trudy was sending him. Looking up at Priest, he handed him the phone. Then he turned to Deke. "Maybe he doesn't have a choice."

Deke frowned and glanced at Sam and Mountain. "What the fuck does that mean? He doesn't have a choice? Everyone has a choice."

"Trudy dug into his past and Breaker has a fifteen-year-old daughter, named Amy and right now Amy is missing," Priest informed him.

Deke looked over at his father and the other men. "And just how does Trudy know this?"

Priest turned the phone over to Deke.

He read the information Trudy sent them. It was a police report from the Concord PD. Kyle and Janice Ruppert's home had been invaded and Janice was injured. She had been almost murdered, in fact she was still in hospital, and Kyle had been beaten. He also reported his fifteen-year-old daughter was missing. He didn't see who invaded his home but neighbors had given statements that the men who broke into their home left on motorcycles.

Deke slowly ran his fingers through his hair. Looking over at Priest he asked, "Why wouldn't he mention this?"

"If Buckley has his daughter he might be under duress but it's still a lie," Sam argued. "He's still betraying the MC, no matter which way you fucking slice it."

"Sam," Black Jack interjected. "He's fighting to keep his little girl alive."

Priest looked thoughtful for a moment then asked, "How did we find out about the four men in Lowell?"

"Breaker told us about them. Why?" Deke narrowed his eyes.

"Maybe he didn't betray the MC after all," Bane informed them.

"How do you figure that old man?" Deke growled.

"Well, think about it..." Bane explained. "He couldn't come right out and tell you what was going on. He has to protect his kid, but by telling you about the guys waiting for Buckley, he knew we'd find these plans and be able to close off the tunnel before they get here."

"That doesn't get his daughter back now does it?" Deke grumbled.

"Maybe that's what his brothers are for," Priest commented.

Deke snapped his head around to Priest. "And just why would his brothers help him? He was willing to give them up to a murderer."

"And just how far would you go to get your own daughter back from a mad man?" Sam asked his son.

Deke lost his belligerent attitude. He'd die for his children and Cassie. He'd kill for them if the need ever rose. He glared at his father. "He has little to no expectation his daughter is still alive. That report is over a week old."

"He's probably living on hope and a prayer but don't you think he knows Amy might not be alive anymore?" Sam shook his head. "He knows and he also knows that Buckley has a bullet with his name on it. He remembers Bear and he knows how those two boys grew up. He knows exactly what kind of man Oscar Buckley is."

"So how do we confront him?" Deke looked livid.

"How about straight on?" Mountain suggested. "He's got to know we would figure this out anyway. If he sent us to Lowell, he must have known we'd get this info."

Deke turned to look at Priest. "How did you find out about the men in Lowell?"

Priest looked over at James and nodded at the man. "James found the information and dug into the rumors then brought the information to me. We dug a little deeper and confirmed it, then brought it to you."

Every eye in the room turned to James.

He raised an eyebrow and stared back at them, then broke the uncomfortable silence filling the room, "I was contacted on an old email address. He and I had several untraceables as a buffer between us and the rest of the world. I usually don't look into each job that's offered but for some reason this one stuck out. I contacted the mark and he told me some things I couldn't believe. On a hunch, I dug into what he told me and I found it was true. That's when I told Priest about what I heard."

"Do you know who the email was from?" Black Jack asked.

"All I could find was that the address came from a library in Concord, New Hampshire."

Deke looked at his brothers. They all knew Breaker had moved to Concord after he left the MC. He told them all he had a friend he wanted to look up. He said he had family there. He got on the phone and called the clubhouse.

A short time later, there was a knock on the door and when Priest opened it, he found Wiley and Gator standing there.

Behind them was Breaker and he didn't look so good.

Iceman and Deacon were standing behind Breaker. When he hesitated to follow Gator and Wiley into the room Iceman pushed him inside. Breaker stumbled then straightened his walk and turned to face the men he once knew as brothers.

"Did you manage to get here unseen?" Deke asked his men.

Iceman nodded. "We've got our own eyes on the three men James pointed out as belonging to Buckley." Turning to Bane he mentioned, "We've also got eyes on your woman Sarah."

Bane stiffened and frowned. "Why? Why are you watching her?"

"Because we don't know her and we don't know you," Deke replied. "We have to look out for this town and the people who live here, they are our family and you and Sarah are not."

Bane wanted to argue the point but he wasn't ready to give up his new identity yet. He had to play out this part if he hoped to keep Bane and his do over alive.

Deke turned his attention to Breaker. "Well old man, what kind of trouble did you bring back here with you?"

"I have no fucking idea what you're talking about Deke," Breaker stammered.

"Oh yeah you, fuckind do, don't you?" Deke watched as the other man tried to make believe he didn't know what was going on. "What happened that turned you against us?"

Breaker seemed to lose his stature. He ran his hands through his hair and down his face. "I haven't turned on you guys man. Don't ever think that. You gained my allegiance a long time ago and that was for life man."

"Then what the fuck is going on here?" Iceman challenged the other man.

"Tell us what this is about," Deke stated as he shoved the phone in Breaker's face.

When Breaker got a look at the article on the phone screen, he visibly paled. Sweat beaded on his forehead and his hand shook as he reached for the phone. The police report was a week old. Tears rolled down his face as he read the details listed there. "I was late getting home that night. To me, it was just another Tuesday night. I had heard about Oscar and Matty getting out of prison but never thought they would come looking for me. I hadn't thought about Bear in years.

Anyway, when I got home I found my front door kicked in and my wife Katie on the floor." He glared at Deke and snarled, "Those fuckers beat her almost to death then they walked away leaving her gasping for air and laying in a pool of her own fucking blood." Taking a deep breath Breaker went on, "Matty stayed behind. He told me I had a beautiful daughter and how bad he felt about having to beat my old lady." Shrugging Breaker went on to say, "He told me that now was the time to reaffirm my vows of loyalty to Bear. I told him Bear was dead and had been for some time. Matty laughed and then he told me he knew that and that the world might be better off without him still here but that when I took his brother's life that day, I lost my own. I didn't get to have a happy ever after. He and his dad were going to make sure of that. He motioned to my wife and said she was a tough nut to crack but they finally got her to shut up. Then he looked around my house and said I had a decent life here but it was going to be a pleasure to take it all away from me. They were going to leave me with nothing, the same as they had. The bastard told me I should forget about my kid cuz I'd never see her in one piece again. I broke then. I asked him what they wanted."

Then men in the room looked angry as they listened.

Breaker ran his fingers through his hair again. Looking over at Deke he whispered, "He offered me one way to get my girl a few more days on this earth. He said she might even live long enough to watch his dad put the bullet in my head." He held out his hands in surrender. "All I had to do was get inside and open the tunnel door for them."

"And you would have let us put our families in the basement for their safety when Buckley and his gang came to call wouldn't you?" Iceman growled.

Breaker swirled around to face him. "No, I wouldn't have done that. You have to believe me. I never would have done that." He crumbled and sat down hard on the sofa. Looking a little lost, he stared at his weathered hands. "I held my Katie in these hands until the ambulance came and I held her hand all the way to the hospital. Her blood stained my hands as the doctors worked on her. They were still stained after they put her in the ICU and then they held her hand when she breathed her last breath," he ended up in a whisper.

No one spoke for the next few minutes.

Then Breaker raised his head and glared at Deke. "Those bastards beat my Katie to death, I'll be damned if I'll turn my back on my daughter. You do what you have to do to save the club but I'm going after my little girl."

"And just how are you going to get to her on the road?" Wiley asked. "She might not even be with them. Those men are riding to start a war with us, they'd be foolish to bring her with them. And there's a whole lot of road between Concord and here. She could be anywhere." He paused and suggested, "She might even be dead already. You have to admit that much."

Breaker nodded even with tears rolling down his weathered face. "Yes, I know that. The odds aren't real good but until I know for sure, I have to hope she's still alive. She's a little too much like her old man to give up that quick."

"Did you know about the tunnel when Bear was still President here?" Deke asked.

Breaker shrugged. "We all did. That tunnel was our storage place. We moved dope and guns through this town. The cops knew it, the people knew it, but they could never find where we stored them. The cops never found the tunnel and we used it for years before you all got here. Then after Bear was killed, we continued to use it until we ran out of dope and guns. Then when you changed our course and we went legit, we no longer had to use it so we closed it up. It's been closed now for about sixteen years." Shrugging he shook his head. "Oscar and Matty were never here when Bear was President so how the hell did they even know about the tunnel?"

"Maybe one of the other men from the MC?" Deke suggested.

"It's possible but I don't think so. When I said we all knew about the tunnel I wasn't talking about every member of the MC." Shaking his head, Breaker continued, "The only ones that really knew about it were the council, the President, the VP, the two Sergeant at arms, the enforcers and the treasurer. Only seven men. Bear was president and he's dead, there was me and Riley and Tate, Jerry and Paulie and Stuart."

"Then it has to be one of them," Sam swore.

Breaker shook his head. "Riley and Tate moved on to another MC and I heard both of them were killed in a standoff with the police on a drug run. Jerry, Paulie and Stuart were dead within the five year limit you set for all of us when you took over. Paulie overdosed in a small town two years after he left. Stuart was killed in a shootout with cops over in Albany and Jerry went to prison when he got caught selling to an undercover cop four years ago. He got into some sort of trouble inside and ended up getting shived. Now he's in a wheelchair for the rest of his life."

James turned to Priest. "Buckley got additional years inside for shiving another prisoner. Left him in a wheelchair for the rest of his life."

"That mother fucker!" Breaker swore as he soared to his feet. "I'm gonna kill that bastard. He must have told Oscar everything he knew. Hell, he probably even told him it was me that shot Bear. That's why they killed my wife and took my kid. They were never going to let her go."

"So, what are we going to do about this?" Iceman asked the difficult question.

"We're gonna to catch them with their pants down." Deke growled.

Breaker shook his head. "There's something else here you need to know."

Deke whirled around to glare at him. "Like what?"

"I'm not the only one here to set you up. I may not be here for Buckley but there are others who are." Breaker straightened his shoulders and faced his President. "Buckley has four men watching you and watching me."

Deke swung his eyes to Priest and then back to Breaker. "We found three men but not the fourth. Are you sure of the numbers?"

Breaker nodded. "I watched all four ride out. They were to be Buckley's eyes and ears here until he got his MC together. They were going to keep an eye on you and me to make sure I did what I was supposed to do."

Deke looked around at the men assembled with him then turned his steel-like gaze to James. "You missed a man." Turning back to Breaker he asked, "When will Buckley get here? Did he have a date set for you to have the door opened?"

Breaker nodded. "Yeah, he wanted the door opened by Saturday. He hoped to catch you all unaware. He thought he would come in while you guys were drinking and partying."

"Why would we be partying on Saturday?" Sam asked.

"Well, normal MC's like to party on the weekends." Breaker shook his head.

"Doesn't matter." Deke growled. "Today is Thursday we only have two days to get this locked down."

"Lock it down?" Breaker pondered. "How the fuck are you going to lock this down? Buckley is coming to start a fucking war and kill every man, woman and child in your MC. How the hell do you prepare for that or lock that down?"

Deke grabbed Breaker's shirt and hauled him in close. He glared eye to eye at the other man. He was so tightly wound his massive arms ballooned as his muscled bunched under his skin. "You have no idea what we can and cannot do. My men will protect not only their MC but their families as well and they will stand shoulder to shoulder to protect this town. Buckley may think he knows what we're going to do but he has no fucking clue what he's coming into."

Deke turned to James. "We need to find that fourth man. I can get Amos and his men to find where they're staying but we need to know if they have any communication going on with Buckley. We'll set up a net over this town, if anything happens we'll know about it." He turned to Breaker. Poking the man in the chest he growled, "You are going to show us this fucking tunnel, both ends of it. Is there anything else, any other secrets about the clubhouse we need to know about? If there is, share them now. I will not be caught unaware again."

"The tunnel isn't just a one-way tunnel," Breaker told them. "It's more of an underground series of tunnels. Bear wouldn't let us down there a lot but he often spoke of other tunnels and storage rooms off the main line. When we had dope and guns down there, he always had at least one man down there on guard. Toward the end there, Bear was getting paranoid about what was hidden in the tunnels." Breaker shrugged. "I thought we emptied it all out after you took over but when Matty stayed behind to let me know he took my kid he said something about finally getting his hands on Bear's treasure."

"Bear's treasure?" Sam asked.

Breaker nodded. "Yeah, it was something Oscar had Bear hold onto for him, something like an inheritance or something like that. Matty said it was something that his father took a long time ago and that Bear had been holding it for Oscar while he served his time. He said it should be worth a pretty penny by this time and would be completely solid by now. The cops couldn't trace it back to them anymore."

Deke raised an eyebrow at the other man's words. He nodded at Priest and this stranger, Theo. "We will be in touch."

His men followed him out and they took Breaker with them.

Bane met Priest's gaze. "Well, that went about as well as a hangover after a car accident."

Priest shrugged. "We knew he wouldn't take it well. Now onto our next step."

Chapter Six

Deke had no clue what Breaker was talking about but once the threat was neutralized, he would search the tunnel system below the ground and hopefully find what treasure was hidden from the world all this time.

He'd called Amos to get his men sent out to cover the city. Amos' men could cover the city and no one would know they were there. He also needed them to follow the three men working for Buckley and report where they were holed up. He needed to know where this fourth man was hiding and how they were communicating with Oscar Buckley.

An hour later, Deke pulled into the compound. He knew the others were already there but he had a stop to make on his way home. As he shut down his bike, he looked around the one and only place he'd called home.

Growing up with his mother, they had lived in a crummy trailer but it never felt like home. She was either working long hours or out with a line of men she never brought back to where they lived. Whatever the reason, he never saw her.

Then when Sam took him home with him, Deke never felt their house in Bangor was home either. Sam was more into his MC life than he was into fathering Deke. He always felt second best with Sam.

It was only when he, Gator and Reva left Maine and came here that Deke felt at home. Coming to Troy was the best thing that happened to him and he never regretted it. Looking around the place he had come to love, he thought back seventeen years.

He'd been so young back then. When he saw this MC, he wanted to stay but he just couldn't live under Bear's rule. While he hadn't been the one to take out the old President he felt he had earned the title stitched on his cut. It had been Deke that turned the MC around, throwing out the dope dealers and the gun runners he made this MC into something he felt very proud of.

They had not only gone legit but had grown over the years to the point this town needed them. He vowed he would never let them down or let them fall under Oscar Buckley's rule. Oscar would be worse than living under Bear's rule. And he'd be damned if after all this time, he would allow the MC to fall backwards instead of pushing forward.

His stop had been to let the network know what was coming to Troy. Amos and his men had been watching the three men James had pointed out. They really did have a finger on the pulse of this town. Amos told him once they had claimed this town as their own and they would always protect it.

Like them, Deke vowed not to give up or give in to the demands of Oscar Buckley. He wanted to bring a war to this town, then Deke would give him a war but he'd be damned if he'd let the likes of Oscar Buckley win it.

~*~

It was barely dawn when Deke heard someone pounding on his front door. Groaning, he got out of bed without disturbing Cassie and stomped his way to the door. Throwing it open, he glared at the man standing on the other side. "What the hell do you want at this fucking hour?"

Zipper stared at him seemingly unafraid of the bluster from his president. "We got more info you need to know."

Deke blew out his breath and nodded. Running his hands through his rumpled hair, he replied, "Give me a minute to get dressed and I'll meet you at the clubhouse." He closed the door and turned to find his wife standing there with a worried look on her face.

"What's going on Deke?" she asked softly.

Deke sighed. He'd hoped not to worry her about this but knew he couldn't keep her in the dark. She had a right to know what could be going down. "Baby, we got a war coming. I want you to pack up the kids and go somewhere you'll be safe for a couple of days until this is over."

Cassie shook her head. "No way. I'm not leaving my home for some piece of shit to come here and take over. No way."

"Honey, this man is looking to kill every man, woman and child who lives behind these walls. I don't want him to spill your blood or the blood of my kids. I'd rather see you and the kids' safe than have to worry about what's happening to you."

"I'm not leaving, Deke," she told him again. "This is my home too. Probably the only one I've ever had." She moved closer to him and touched his bare chest. "I love you and I will not leave this place just to be safe while you face this monster. I've been hearing word on the streets about this Buckley asshole. It's not a secret and hasn't been for a couple of days now. People still remember the days when Bear ruled this compound."

"People?" Deke quirked an eyebrow.

She smiled slightly. "Amos and Frankie and some of the older guys around town. Amos came to me yesterday and started asking questions I didn't have answers for. Then he began telling me about what happened here before you and your guys came to town. They didn't have a good life before you got here but after Bear was killed, they stayed to see what you would do. They watched and waited and finally believed you would be good for this town."

Deke nodded. "I know. I stopped in and spoke to Amos and Frankie last night. They told me pretty much the same thing. I was most surprised to find out they'd been living here that long." Shaking his head he told her, "They had noticed pretty much the same thing this James guy found, they knew the three men were already here. They've been watching them since they got here. Amos told me where they were staying and the fact there might be one more man linked to them."

"So what's going on and why is Bear's family coming here to start up trouble?"

"We think there's something hidden in those tunnels that Buckley still wants to collect. Something no one but him knows about."

Cassie shook her head. "What else is there that you aren't telling me?"

"Breaker, the man that came here a few days ago was here when I first got here to Troy. When I came here seventeen years ago with Gator and Reva, Breaker was VP under Bear. The club was so different back then. They ran this town with an iron hand and the people living here were afraid of them. They ran drugs, guns and plenty of other illegal shit. Even though the town felt like home to me, I couldn't stay here. I was about to pull out when the incident happened that put me in as the leader of this crew. You know I got blamed for taking over the club when Bear was killed, right?"

Cassie nodded.

"Well, I'm not the one who pulled the trigger on the bastard, Breaker did that. He stayed for a while under my presidency but then he felt he was too old for an MC. He claimed it was time for him to settle down and have a family. That wouldn't have been possible under Bear's rule but he knew I would be different and we left on good terms. He settled in Concord and got what he wanted. A family. He admitted to us he had a wife and a daughter. Buckley just got out of prison after spending thirty years for crimes he committed. Matty only spent the last ten years or so behind bars and the first thing Oscar did was get some men together. He's coming back here to take back the MC we set up a long time ago. What we didn't know until last night was the fact that Buckley made a stop in Concord to invade Breaker's home, where he beat the wife to death and took his young daughter hostage. They're using her to keep Breaker in line."

"What did they want him to do?" Cassie asked.

"To gather every member of the MC in the Club house and then to open the tunnel for them to be able to get inside without having to come through the front gate. They planned to murder our whole MC, men, women and children. Then just take over everything we have set up. They'll bring back the drugs and guns and whatever else they can. They will run wild over this town and shoot anyone who tries to stop them."

Deke spelled it out for her and Cassie couldn't imagine anything worse than this. "You can't let that happen." She gasped.

"I don't plan on it," Deke assured her.

"What are you going to do?"

"I'm going to go down into the tunnels and find what Bear hid for his father and then I'm going to catch Buckley out in the open. It may get bloody but I hope it's their blood spilling not ours." Shaking his head Deke looked at her. "I was hoping you and the rest of the wives and kids were in a safe place but I have a feeling that isn't going to happen is it?"

Cassie smiled. "No it isn't. We live here too. We have the right to protect the place we call home too."

"Damn woman," he swore. "The boys have some news I need to hear. Why don't you get the kids up and come down to the clubhouse. I think I'd feel better with you where I can see you rather than alone here."

"Ok, we'll be right behind you," Cassie agreed rather quickly.

Deke shook his head. "No, just get them ready and I'll send one of the boys to escort you all to the clubhouse. In fact, I'll call one of the boys to wait for you."

"Is that really necessary?" Cassie asked. "Surely, we're safe on the compound grounds?"

Deke walked closer and brushed a strand of hair from her forehead. "Cassie, you and those babies mean the world to me. I would die or kill any threat to you, if I had to. If something ever happened to you or them, I would never live through it. I know you think this is overkill but this is what I need to keep my mind right."

Cassie reached out and cupped his jaw in a caress. "Ok, I get what you're saying and I'll do what you want, just don't ask me or any of the other wives to leave here. We can't and won't leave our men behind just to save our own lives. Don't you all know we can't survive without you? We wouldn't want to even try."

Deke took her hand from his face and cupping her hand, he pressed a kiss into her palm. "Ok, but I do want to keep you girls as safe as we can until this threat is gone."

"Then let's get the kids and get down to the club so you can discuss what you need to do." She turned to wake their children while Deke got someone on the phone to collect his family and bring them into safety.

A short time later, he kissed his wife and kids then told them he'd see them when they got to the clubhouse. Walking down the path, he didn't notice anything out of the ordinary. When he reached the backdoor, he pushed it open and the whole clubhouse grew quiet.

Zipper was busy working his computer as Gator, Reva and the others were standing around the main room. When he walked in, Gator joined him along with Sam and Breaker. Mountain, Black Jack and a few others came over as well.

"Ok what's going on?" Deke asked the group of men.

"Amos called in that more riders arrived after we met," Gator explained. "His men are watching the roads coming and going from Troy. They must have gotten to Lowell and found the rest of their group missing. Buckley pushed on through with the men they had at hand."

Zipper came over and handed Deke some paperwork.

Deke scanned the papers and raised his eyes to Gator. Handing the pages over, he turned to Zipper. "Is this for real?"

Zipper nodded. "Trudy emailed this info to me an hour ago. I had to verify it before I came to you."

Gator whistled when he read the reports in his hand. Looking up, he asked, "Are you freakin kidding me? Oscar was suspected in three high end bank robberies, back to back bank robberies, not to mention robbing an armored truck hauling diamonds into Wall Street?"

Breaker slapped his forehead. "Wow, that's what it was."

Deke turned to look at him. "What?"

Breaker turned to stare him down. "The Satan's Spawn MC was founded twenty two years ago. We were just a group of bikers back then. We wanted to be but we didn't know how. Then Bear came around and sort of took over our little group. He made a lot of promises and tried to keep them but with everything he did, it came with a cost. He had plenty of money to spend and boy, did he spend it. He tore the old clubhouse down and built this one. He put up the fence around the property to keep everyone else out. He wanted only the club and its members to be allowed inside the walls he built. Then he brought in the drugs and the guns. He made the deals with the cartels to distribute their products. He made good money not only for himself but for us too. Although he took forty percent off the top, he paid us well enough."

Deke crossed his arms over his chest and listened.

"As members, we grew to know he was the boss. We let a lot slide because if we upset the cart, we knew we could end up dead or tossed out with nothing. Bear was getting out of control but we weren't willing to stop him until you gave us a choice." Breaker broke off his spiel to look around the room. "You turned the MC around. You got rid of the riff raff that we'd blossomed into and kept the best of us. You demanded we get our shit together and because of you, we did that. You never demanded more of us then you were willing to do yourself and that set the track for the future. I knew the club would be ok after that. I knew I could leave and start my own life with my Katie and have a good future with her." He raised his hands in the air. "Then this shit happened and brought back all the bad that was Bear."

"That doesn't explain what you were talking about before," Gator reminded him.

Breaker nodded. "I don't think Buckley's money is here anymore. I think Bear spent it all and then some."

"Oh, that's gonna piss papa off, right down to his black soul." Wiley shook his head.

Before Deke could say anything, the back door opened. He turned his head and saw Cassie and the kids come in. He expelled a deep breath and settled his calm. At least she was here under his watch and he could concentrate on other things. He turned back to the men. "We need to find out what's down in that tunnel and what's not. After we find out what's what, then we can make plans to protect what's ours." He turned to Mountain. "I want patrols walking the fence line and I want guards posted."

Mountain nodded. "I'll get right on that. Izzy is on her way over with Danny. I tried to talk her into going to visit her father for a few days but she told me in no uncertain terms, no way."

Deke shook his head. "Yeah, I got the same argument from Cassie."

Sam snorted. "Yeah, Melora said the same thing. This is her home and she'll be damned if she's gonna be forced out of it."

Deke smiled. "The women of this MC are not giving up as easy as we would think huh?"

Sam slapped Deke on the back. "Son, they are here to stay the same as we are. You'd better believe they aren't going anywhere."

"Then we need to get them behind these walls where we can keep an eye on them." Exhaling slowly he stated, "Let's go find out what's left of Bear's money pot. We need to find out if he left anything for his dad."

Breaker led the way to the basement. Footsteps followed him down the wooden stairs and when he went over to the wall he pushed a secret block of cement and the entire wall opened up to reveal the entrance of the tunnel hidden underground.

With the wall opened up the entire basement doubled in size and the opened area was filled with seventeen years of dust and cobwebs. Breaker coughed as the dust flew up and into his face. He waved the dust away and peered down the dark tunnel. When a flashlight was pressed into his hands, he moved forward into the tunnel and flipped a switch. Then the lights flickered and lit up the stone walls.

The men gathered around and let Breaker lead the way. He went all the way down the long tunnel before he stopped outside one of the many doors along the way. He pushed the door open and they could all see the contents of the area. There was an open safe in the room along with a small wooden table.

The safe was empty and there were bank bands all over the floor. The bands matched the bank robberies and they found several small velvet bags both inside the safe and on the floor.

Deke squatted on his heels and picked up one of the velvet bags. Opening it, he found nothing inside but then he didn't expect to. He knew then the money Oscar trusted his son to keep for him was gone. Looking over his shoulder, he shook his head. "I have a feeling it's a good thing Bear is already dead. I don't think he would have survived a family reunion."

"And now neither will we," Breaker assured him. "If Oscar finds out the money he left with Bear is gone, he's gonna be so pissed off he won't care who lives or dies."

"We have to get everyone back here and on lock down," Deke told them. "Call your women and gather your families here. We'll find room for them but we need to get them under our eyes."

"What about the men watching our businesses?" Mountain asked. "Won't that tip them off?"

Deke got to his feet and faced his men. "By now, Oscar must know we would have found out about his pending visit. He's not stupid. His men aren't stupid. He must have made promises they will expect him to keep. If he can't, then he's going to have to face them too. Now with what we know about the men riding with him, they won't take the news well."

Mountain huffed. "He'll be lucky if one of his own men doesn't put a bullet in his head."

"Unless he thinks you found the tunnel and the money, then you all will be in danger. He won't stop until he gets it all back," Breaker interjected. "He's still got my daughter and if I betray him, he'll kill her right in front of me."

"Well, we can speculate all we want but until we face him man to man, or face to face we won't know what's going to happen," Deke suggested. "We may or may not have time left to gather our families and get ready for them. We aren't going to run and we aren't going to hide. We'll face them head on but we will face them. We have to." He turned and made his way back to the main room.

One by one, his men joined him and when they were all gathered there the front door opened as Priest and James joined them.

"What are you doing here?" Deke asked.

"We have news that couldn't wait." Priest looked troubled.

Deke closed his eyes and sighed deeply. "Ok, hit me with it."

"We found them. They arrived at the shack where they were supposed to meet with the last four men last night. They were not happy when the men were not there to meet them."

"And how do you know that?" Sam asked.

Priest looked over at James and stated, "James put up a camera and we were able to watch them arrive."

"We also watched the fit Oscar threw when he realized they weren't there," James said dryly. "He was particularly pissed when he didn't find the tunnel plans or the clubhouse plans. He now has no clue where to find us or how to find the tunnel. When he comes here, he's going to be looking for a way in. He isn't going to care if it's through the front gate or the tunnel."

Deke closed his eyes and groaned. "Well, we have news too. We found out Oscar used to rob banks before he went to prison and he left his haul in what he thought were safe hands with Bear. All Bear had to do was keep it safe for his dad when he got out of prison, instead Bear blew the whole works. There isn't anything left for Daddy to build his own MC with."

Priest nodded. "Yeah, we got the same word from Trudy. We didn't know there wasn't anything left though." He glanced over at James. Then he looked over at Breaker. "We found evidence that your daughter is still alive. She's a little roughed up but she's still alive."

"But for how long?" Breaker groaned. "When Oscar can't find the tunnel, he'll make her the centerpiece of his entrance into the compound. Then when he's inside, he'll spill her blood just the same as he'll spill yours."

"You don't know that." Sam shook his head.

Breaker barked out a laugh. "You didn't see the look in that bastard's eyes when he left with her. His eyes were cold as ice and dark as hell itself."

"What if we could get her away from them?" Bane asked.

"Just how do you plan on doing that?" Breaker dared to whisper.

"Oh, we are by no means done here yet, gentlemen," Bane assured them. "We may be down a bit but we aren't out just yet. Not by a long shot. We can still turn this around and come out on top."

Chapter Seven

James turned to Deke and Priest. "Can we talk in private for a moment?" he asked in a low voice.

Deke stared at the other man for a second then turned and led the way down the hall to his office. Opening the door, he ushered the other men inside.

When he went to close the door, Sam pushed it open again and joined them. He stood with his back to the door.

James looked over at Deke. "I was asked to dig into a man by the name of Jack Connors and I'll admit I found out some very disturbing things regarding the man."

"Who asked about him?" Deke frowned.

"Bane asked me to look into it."

"Why? Who is this Jack Connors?" Deke wanted to know.

"He's Sarah's stepfather," James informed them.

"And?" Sam asked with a frown.

"And I found out Jack was killed fourteen years ago. Actually, he was murdered with a baseball bat. The only people home at the time of his death were his wife Ellen and his stepdaughter Sadie Masterson."

Sam pushed himself away from the wall and stomped over to the other men. "Sadie Masterson? Are you sure that's her name?"

James nodded.

Sam turned to Priest. "Did you know about this?"

Priest shrugged. "Not until today. That's why we're telling you and Deke about this."

Deke looked at his father and then over to the man he knew as Priest. "What's this all about? Who is Sadie Masterson? And why is this so alarming?"

Sam snapped his head around to where his son was standing. "Sadie Masterson is Stone Masterson's little sister. You might know him as Pappy."

"What the hell is she doing here?" Deke asked, shocked.

"She ran away when she was fifteen and he's been looking for her for years," Sam informed him. "You know I've been friends with Pappy for most of my adult life. I have to tell him. I owe him my life in fact."

"What are you going to do?" Deke asked his dad.

"He needs to know where she is and what's about to come down." Sam gritted his teeth. "He needs to know before anything happens to her or if she takes off again."

"Yeah, well she mentioned something else about Jack Connors." James interrupted Sam's rant. "She said something about Jack's three brothers and his father looking for her or her mother. She seems to think they want her to pay for killing Jack. No one knows what happened that night, only that Jack's head came into contact with a bat. They don't know who swung it or why and I think they really want answers. They also want revenge and they will continue to search for her until they find her."

Sam shook his head. "That doesn't sound good." He glanced over at Priest. "If you don't call him, I will."

Priest tipped his head. "Feel free to make the call. I might know the man but you have a different kind of history with him. It might be better coming from you rather than me."

Sam nodded. Then he looked back at James. "Just where do the Connors brothers hail from? And how hard are they looking for Sadie?"

"They live in Saratoga Springs and they've had five P.I.'s looking all over the state for her in the last fourteen years."

"Where did her mother end up? I know Sadie relocated her then left her behind as she was afraid to stay and draw attention to her."

"Mrs. Connors moved to Sidney, New York. She is living under the name of Mrs. Stone and working in the police department."

"Do we have any idea where Buckley is right now?" Deke couldn't stay away from the topic very long.

"He is presently in Palmer, Massachusetts. He's waiting for his men to catch up."

"And you know this how?" Deke asked.

"We tagged their bikes."

Deke nodded and looked over at his dad. "You'd better make that call before Stone loses his sister for good. We'll try to protect her but she may get caught in the crossfire." Shaking his head he said, "I don't want that to happen but any of us can get caught in the crossfire. Those bastards don't care who they have to go through."

Priest nodded. "Theo said that he and Sarah will be here in a few minutes."

Sam growled and reached for his phone. Making this call right now was no problem for him, he just didn't want Pappy's reunion with his sister to be short lived or not happen at all.

~*~

When a call came in on his cell phone, Pappy answered it without looking at the caller ID. Not many people knew this number so whoever was on the other end he knew. When he heard Sam Tory's voice, he grinned. "What the hell do you want Tory?" he growled with a grin.

"Captain, I got some news you've been wanting for some time now," Sam greeted him.

"Oh, yeah?" Pappy leaned back in his chair, intrigued. "And what news would that be?"

"Do you remember when we rescued Cricket and Deke's daughter at that cabin at Saranac Lake?"

Pappy sighed hard. "Yeah, I remember. What about it?"

"You told me something you were looking for, your sister Sadie, do you remember?"

Pappy could barely speak, as the lump in his throat was so big. "I remember. What about it?"

"I found her. She's here in Troy right this minute."

Pappy sat forward in his chair so fast he almost fell on the floor. "Are you sure it's Sadie?"

"I'm sure. She's with a man called Theo. Don't worry Priest knows him and trusts him." Sam sighed heavily. "But we got trouble coming and it's gonna be bad trouble. We might not live through it. I just wanted you to know in case we don't make it."

"Don't you let anything happen to her until I get there, Gunny." Pappy called him the name Sam had used while in the Military. "I'm on my way. Don't you let her run either. I have to know she's ok."

"We'll keep her here Pappy. But if you're coming, you'd better hurry."

"What you got going on Gunny?" Pappy frowned.

"A man looking for trouble and willing to kill every man, woman and kid here at our MC to get through the front gate. It's not good. What he's after is no longer here and hasn't been for a long time."

"I'm on my way. Hold the fort down and wait for me." Pappy disconnected the call and rushed down the hall to the main room of his clubhouse. Seeing his men, he grinned and announced, "Who wants to play some games with the enemy?"

His men rose to their feet one at a time. "What's up Pappy?"

"We got an MC in trouble and I may have found my sister. She's right in the thick of it, so I have to go play big brother and take out some bad guys. Anybody want to go with me?"

"Hell yeah we do!" they all called out. "When do we leave?"

"Well, Bastian said his plane was at our disposal so get your war gear packed up. We leave in thirty minutes. Time's a wastin guys."

Then he saw his wife standing in the kitchen doorway. Her eyes told him more than her body language. She looked worried but resigned to the fact he was going off to fight another war. He walked over to her and gently brushed a strand of hair away from her face.

"Sweetheart, I have to go and find out if this is really Sadie. If it is, she's in big trouble and I have to try to save her."

McKenna smiled and cupped his jaw. "I know you have to go, just make sure you come back home again."

"I will sweetheart. I will. Nothing could drag me away from what I got here." He gathered her in his arms and pressed his lips to hers. Blood rushed to the lower part of his body as he groaned and pushed her away. "Darlin, as much as I want to finish this I have to get my gear and get on a plane. Sam Tory said they got trouble in New York and if I want to see Sadie again, I'd better get there before all hell breaks loose."

McKenna smiled and kissed him gently. "You go and make this world a better place to live in. When you come back, bring your sister with you. I'd like to meet her."

Pappy kissed her again, then turned and walked away.

A couple of hours later a plane touched down and taxied to the terminal. A lone man stood waiting for the men who walked off the plane. Sam grinned at the number of men who had joined Pappy on this trip. He counted a dozen men and all had their battle gears with them. Sam's grin widened as they all came in and met him. "Hell Pappy, if I knew you were bringing the troops with ya, I would have ordered a van instead of bringing my truck."

Pappy grinned. "We'll make due Gunny. Let's get back so you can fill us in with the threat against the MC. We can only deal with one thing at a time. Besides, I want to see Sadie again." Running his finger over his head, he looked a bit green around the gill. "I haven't seen her in many years." He looked over at Sam. "Is she ok? This guy she's with, is he treating her right?"

Sam snorted. "I'll let you see for yourself. I'm not going to say anything about that." He paused and added, "But yeah Pappy, he treats her well."

"Well then, let's get on the road and you can explain what's going on." Pappy urged. They turned and followed Sam out to the parking lot. Sam, Pappy and Dewey got in the cab while everyone else sat down in the back of the pickup. It was a good thing the clubhouse was only fifteen minutes away and Sam took the back roads to get there. It sure would look funny to some, having men looking like these did, in the back of a truck.

When they arrived, Wiley opened the gate and watched in amazement as he watched the truck pull in. The additional men would be welcome in the upcoming fight.

Gator joined him and he watched the men unloading the back of Sam's truck while Wiley turned to lock the gate. The silence was shattered when a single gunshot rang out.

Everyone ducked and began searching the area.

Only Wiley saw Gator crumble first to his knees then all the way to the ground. Wiley's eyes widened in horror as he saw the red stain on Gator's chest. He turned his head and bellowed for Deke.

Deke came running out of the clubhouse right past his dad and the group of men kneeling in the dirt. Another shot rang out and a puff of dirt rose just in front of Deke as he ran over to his friend. Skidding to his knees, he took in the situation in an instant. He motioned for Wiley to help him drag Gator back to the clubhouse.

Within seconds, they had men on either side of them giving them cover fire. Deke grabbed Gator's right arm while Wiley grabbed his left, curling their bodies over the wounded man they began dragging him, then their burden was lifted as two more men picked up his legs and they carried him quickly to the shelter of the main clubhouse.

Sam was at the door and he held it open as Deke, Wiley and the other two men rushed inside.

Reva rushed forward and cleared off a table so they could lay her man down.

Raine rushed out of the back room with his medic kit and took a quick assessment of what he was dealing with. He dug into the kit and grabbed his scissors.

Deke wrestled Gator's vest off his shoulders and watched as Raine cut his t shirt off. The hole in his chest was pulsing fresh blood with each beat of Gator's heart. His face looked pale and his skin was growing cold.

Cassie, Peaches, Sarah and several of the other women all stood to one side hugging while they watched Raine working on Gator. One of Pappy's men pushed through the crowd and began working beside Raine. Digging into the medic kit, he began lining up the instruments Raine would need to dig out the bullet and then close the wound. Raine didn't question or argue as the tools he needed were handed to him when he needed them.

Instead, he dug out the bullet and cleaned up the wound. The only sound that anyone heard in the room was the soft sobbing from Reva as she watched the man she loved fighting for his life. Raine and the other man worked together very well and soon Raine was closing the wound on Gator's chest. He stepped back and Reva was there to grab her husband's hands like she would never give it up again. She placed her other hand over his heart so he would feel her but mostly so she would feel his own heartbeat.

Raine and his medic buddy stepped into the kitchen Deke, Pappy, Sam and Mountain followed. Raine was angry as he scrubbed his hands and lower arms. The other man watched as he washed up. He kept looking over at Pappy.

Finally, Raine turned the water off and grabbing a dish towel he turned to look at Deke.

"Well? Is he gonna make it?" Deke barked out.

"I don't know," Raine admitted as he dried his hands. "I got the bullet out but he could be bleeding internally and he's lost a lot of blood. He'll need time and possibly a blood transfusion to survive. Hell, he needs a real doctor not a field medic. The next two days will tell if he'll live or not."

Deke ran his hands over his head and growled. "Yeah, but you're all we got right now and I'm not taking any chances moving him." He turned to the others and asked, "Did anyone see where that bullet came from?"

"No, we didn't." Sam growled.

"Does this have anything to do with Oscar Buckley?" Pappy asked.

"It has everything to do with Buckley." Deke gritted as he ran his hands over his hair. Then he shook his head and reached out his hand. "I'm glad to see you Pappy, especially under these circumstances."

Pappy snorted. "Well, Gunny did say there was a threat to the MC. I just didn't know it would come up the minute we got here." He looked around the room then turned to Deke. "If you don't mind, I'll get my men with your men and get them on alert. They might be able to smoke out your sniper."

Deke nodded.

Watching Pappy leave and hearing him barking out orders to his men, he returned a few minutes later. He glanced over at his man and introduced him to the other. "This is my medic, we call him Doc."

Raine turned and held out his hand. "Thank you for your assistance. You saved me time and that could have been critical back then. Hopefully we won't need to work together any more but I'll be glad you're there if we do."

Doc nodded. "No problem. Haven't had to do field surgery in a while and it's always easier when you have someone else there to help." He nodded his head at the other room. "I hope your guy pulls through."

Raine turned and looked at Gator. "It'll be touch and go for a while yet. I hope he pulls through too."

Several other men joined them, including Priest, Bane, James and Dewey Mann.

Priest stepped forward and shook Pappy's hand. "Glad you're here man."

Pappy grinned and said, "Yeah, your plane comes in handy all the time. Especially for quick flights like this one was."

Priest nodded then looked over at Deke.

"Okay, what's the deal here? Why is Oscar Buckley breathing down your neck and what does he want here?" Pappy asked Deke.

"When I got here seventeen years ago, I walked into a mess. The president at the time was a man we all knew as Bear. Bear was a pig. He ran drugs, guns and god only knows what else. He used and abused women. The second night when me and Gator got here, he kidnapped a young woman off the streets of Troy. She was in trouble, but Bear didn't care. He wanted her and not one of his men stood up for her. I did. I beat the everlovin shit out of him when he was going to rape her. I got to him before he could complete the act. I thought it was over but Bear had one little trick up his sleeve. He had a knife I didn't see but his VP did. He put a bullet in Bear's head and after that, I was voted President." Deke took a deep breath and when he exhaled he continued, "Bear's dad and younger brother got out of prison a week ago and they're on their way here to collect a blood debt from us. They want the man who murdered Bear and they want back something Bear was holding for his dad."

"And what would that be?" Pappy asked.

"About three million dollars of bank robbery money and jewels," Deke stated.

Pappy frowned. "Are you sure about the robbery money?"

Sam nodded. "Yeah, we found the evidence. The VP at the time of Bear's death told us about a tunnel we never knew was here. He even showed us where the tunnel is and we've been down there. The thing is Breaker, the old VP, left the club a while back. He had another kind of life in Concord. He had a wife and a little girl. Buckley beat the wife to death and kidnapped Breaker's fifteen-year-old daughter. She's still with him."

"Why would he do that?" Dewey asked.

"Breaker is one of the men still alive when Bear was here. He was one of the handful of men that knew about the tunnel. Buckley told him he wanted him to open the tunnel that would allow them to come into the clubhouse unannounced. Once they got in here, they planned to kill every man, woman and kid here. Buckley plans to just walk into the club's businesses and take over. We aren't about to let him do that." Deke growled. "We were able to stop him from adding numbers to his ragtag group but he's still got about a dozen men with him."

Pappy looked troubled as he listened.

"He's also had three men watching us for about a week now. They may or may not be reporting back to him. But the shooting this morning was the first attempt they've made against us."

Pappy nodded. "I imagine our arrival made them reckless." He looked over at Dewey. "Time must be getting close."

Dewey looked over at Deke and asked, "Is the girl still alive?"

"As far as we know," James told them. "The last we knew was last night. We got to some of the men willing to join him before they did and we took them out. I left a camera and we saw her then, but that was hours ago. Breaker seems to think Buckley will keep her alive long enough to kill her in front of him."

Pappy snorted. "From the info Trudy dug up, that sounds about right. Buckley really is a bastard." Turning to Deke he asked, "So all the money Oscar left with Bear is gone huh? That isn't going to sit well with Dad. That could lead to real trouble. Buckley could flip out completely."

Deke nodded. "Yup, that's the least of our problems. Buckley could rain hell on the innocent people of this city. We can't hide behind these walls if that happens. This is our town, our people." Deke turned to Priest and Bane. "They suggested hitting Buckley before he got here. But we're not killers unless we're pushed into a corner. What they suggested was cold blooded murder." He hesitated then went on, "At least it was until they shot my VP." His face went dark and his eyes went cold. "If they want a fight, they came to the right place."

Sam slapped Pappy on the back. "Looks like you guys got here in the nick of time."

Pappy turned to the man he knew as Theo. When he did, he found Theo staring back. Both men were searching out the other as possible threats to the family. Finally, Pappy asked, "Where is Sadie?"

"I don't know anyone by the name of Sadie," Bane replied. "I do, however, know *a* Sarah. She belongs to me though." He paused, then had to ask, "Is your name Stone?"

Pappy nodded. "I want to see her now."

Bane stared at him for another moment then left the room. When he returned he was with a woman. He pulled her over to Pappy and suggested, "This is my Sarah." Turning to Sarah he asked, "Sarah, do you know this man?"

Sarah trembled as she raised her head to look at her brother for the first time in years. She gasped at the fall of white hair on his head. This threw her for a moment but she melted at the all too familiar look in his blue eyes. "Stone?"

Pappy smiled slightly. "Sadie. Thank God, you're here." He wrapped his big arms around his sister and gently hugged her to him. He saw Bane's glare but he ignored the other man. Finally, Pappy stepped back and gazed at her. He brushed a strand of hair from her forehead and smiled. "I have been looking for you for so long, I didn't know if I would ever find you."

Sarah trembled even more. "You haven't been the only one. I couldn't let anyone find me."

"The Connors?" Pappy's mouth tightened. "Do they know what happened that night? What Jack was going to do to you?"

Sarah shook her head. "They didn't believe the police report. They claimed it was cold blooded murder. They said they couldn't prove which one of us did the deed so they were going to make both of us suffer. I got mom out of there and settled in another town under the protection of the police but I couldn't stay with her."

Pappy nodded. "I found your mom a few years ago. She's just fine but she was worried about you. You were out on the streets far too young and with no word about your being safe it was driving her nuts." He paused then asked, "Why didn't you tell me about what that bastard was doing? About what it was like for you and Mom? Don't you know I would have come home and taken care of that bastard?"

Sarah hung her head. "You were over in a war zone. We didn't tell you because you needed to concentrate on your own business. We didn't want the news to put you or your men in danger. We just couldn't tell you. Mom felt so bad. She admitted she married Jack to stabilize our lives. She said she never loved him, not like she loved our father but she felt we needed a man in our life."

Pappy's lips tightened. "Maybe we did, but we didn't need a man like Jack Connors."

She nodded. "She knew that very quickly in their relationship but by then Jack wouldn't let her go. It wasn't until after you left that he got mean and nasty."

"That's because he knew I'd beat the hell out of him if he touched you or her wrong. He knew I was bigger and stronger than he was even then." Pappy snorted.

Sarah looked up at him with haunted eyes. "I killed him. I hit him with a baseball bat. Mom told me to go to my room and not to come out no matter what I heard. I couldn't stand to hear her screams anymore. I rushed out of my room and just slammed the bat into his head. He'd been standing over her with his hands around her throat. He would have killed her that night if I didn't stop him."

"Then he got what he deserved." Pappy gritted his teeth.

"Stone, I'm so sorry I lied to you about this." Tears rolled down her face. "Can you ever forgive me?"

Pappy softened his expression. "Oh baby girl, I forgive you. Even though I don't like lies, I can overlook this one. You should have trusted me with the truth but I understand why you didn't."

Sarah planted her face in his chest and felt his arm wrap her in a sense of safety she hadn't felt in so long.

Bane pulled her away from her brother. He frowned as he pulled her into his arms. "She's my woman."

"She's my sister." Pappy affirmed her position. "She's been lost to my family for a very long time and if I want to hug her that's something you need to deal with. I understand what you're saying but she was my sister long before she became your woman. You need to understand that."

Bane bared his teeth. "I don't share."

Sarah took a place between the two men, placing one hand on each of their chests. "Please don't start this here. We have a bigger threat to handle. One that none of us may survive. Let's get through that first, then the two of you can have a come to Jesus meeting. But you both have to know, one of you is my past and the other could be my future but you both mean a lot to me and I don't want to lose either of you. So find a way to deal with it." She turned to look at Bane, "I lost everyone who meant anything to me for fourteen very long years. But now I have a chance to get him back into my life and I want that." Turning to face Stone she told him, "Please don't make this harder than it has to be. I love you so much but I have a chance to have a happy ever ending with him. Can you give me a little leeway here? I don't know if he's the one for me or not but I'd like the chance to find out." She walked toward the door of the kitchen. "Can we get back to the problem at hand now?"

Bane turned to Pappy and growled under his breath.

Pappy did the same but both men turned to join the others in the main room.

Chapter Eight

An hour later, one of Pappy's men dragged a man back to the clubhouse. He tossed the man on the floor and looked over at Pappy. "This is the dirtbag that shot your man. He was alone."

Two more of Pappy's men came in and nodded. "We searched the woods but he was the only one we found."

Before anyone could reply, Deke's phone pinged and he reached for it. His eyes never left the man lying on the floor. "Yeah?" he answered as he listened to the conversation. Then he hung up the call and walked over to the downed man. He searched the bruises and cuts on the man as he shook his head. "You are a lucky man my friend."

"Oh, why is that?" He raised an eyebrow.

"You're lucky it wasn't one of my men that found you, you got to live an extra little while." He turned to face the rest of the men standing there. "That was Amos, his men found and contained the other two men on Buckley's payroll. We have a little leeway until the man himself gets here."

The man on the floor looked around and saw Breaker standing on the fringe of the group. His eyes narrowed as he turned to Deke. "You got more problems than Buckley, you fool. You got a traitor amongst your ranks."

Deke turned his head and saw what the other man saw. He turned to him and snarled. "I'd worry more about what we're going to do to you rather than think you got any points to deal with on your side."

The man turned slowly to stare at Deke. "It doesn't matter what you do to me. I just hope I'm still alive to see the life drain out of you when Buckley gets here." Then he turned to glare at Breaker, "Hey old man, I hear your girl is having a great time in Buckley's camp. She's getting her groove on with just about everybody there, even the old man."

Breaker started forward but was held back by more than one man.

The man on the floor snickered and Deke reached out and slammed his fist into his face.

Fresh blood spurted from his broken nose and blood stained his teeth when he smiled. "We'll see who gets the last laugh when Buckley gets here won't we?"

Deke grabbed the man's collar and dragged him to his feet. Shoving him at his men he snarled, "Get this piece of shit out of my sight. Lock him up in the basement in chains. I don't want him to be able to escape. He has a lot to answer for."

Deke watched as his men dragged the prisoner away. Then he looked at Breaker. Studying the other man, he turned to Pappy, then over to James. "Can you let Pappy and his men know where this camp is?"

James nodded. "I know exactly where they are. Men good enough can get in and out easily."

Pappy nodded. "That's what my men do and have done for years. We'll go."

"Then do it, if you're willing." Deke nodded. "Also, take a headcount. I want to know how many men Buckley has with him."

James nodded and turned to gather his intel.

Pappy spoke to several of the men with him.

They all went over to a corner and spoke, as James showed them the info on his laptop.

A few minutes later, Pappy and his men disappeared.

Deke went over to Breaker and clasped his hand on the other man's shoulder. "We'll get her back. Then we'll get her the help she needs to cope with all of this."

Breaker broke down. "How the hell do you come back from this sort of thing? I mean really... *cope*?"

Cassie joined them and held his gaze. "You can learn to cope with anything. Believe me I know, but if she has you and you don't blame her for something you couldn't control, then she can learn to cope. We don't know what happened to her and I'll be damned if I'll take the word of a killer over her own words." She patted his arm. "She'll have us as support for both of you."

Breaker hauled her into his arms and thanked her.

Deke stood there watching the exchange and when Breaker hugged his wife his fingers fisted but he didn't say anything.

Cassie broke their hug and turned to her husband wrapping her arms around his waist. She felt him relax at her touch but neither of them said a word. She let him go and brushed her lips against his. "We can handle what's coming. Together, we can do anything."

She turned and walked back to the group of women waiting on the sidelines. She watched as the men began making plans for the upcoming confrontation with Oscar Buckley.

~*~

Oscar Buckley was frowning while he waited for word from his men. The others were drinking and carousing behind him but he wasn't. The rage usually buried deep within him wanted out and he could almost feel it just under his skin. He was an old man now and he didn't want to be. He'd wasted his younger years behind bars. Thirty years! Thirty fucking years. He couldn't believe it when the judge handed down his sentence. Yeah, he'd killed the bitch he called his wife and yeah he found out later what happened hadn't been her fault but he hadn't felt anything about it. So she hadn't screwed him over this time but there would always be another time.

That didn't really bother him so much anymore, what did bother him was the fact that he trusted his oldest son with his life's work. Three million dollars. He smirked at the thought of finally collecting the money Bear was supposed to keep for him. When he got word of Bear's death seventeen years ago, he'd been outraged.

It had taken some time to find someone who knew the truth about what happened that night but he finally did. He learned from Jerry what happened and the rage he held a tight leash on exploded. When the smoke cleared, Jerry lived but he wasn't the man he once was and Oscar had received ten more years behind bars.

Now, he was out and he'd been busy since his release. Matty joined him and they discussed getting the MC that Bear had back into the family. They had done their research and found the Sin's Bastards were a big thing in Troy.

Oscar snarled when he thought about the good things the MC had done for the town and how he wanted to tear it apart with his bare hands. His boy Bear never would have taken the MC in that direction. He would have ruled that fucking town with fear. Oscar's blood boiled when he thought about what Deke had done to the town and the MC.

He looked over the open fire the guys had going and caught sight of Breaker's girl, Amy. She was scared to death and wore a few bruises due to fighting the men off. When Oscar told the men to leave her alone, she looked almost grateful. His men minded his order but they didn't like it.

Oscar ran a critical eye over his men and shook his head. They were the worst he could find. But they also didn't mind getting their hands dirty and that was what he needed to take control of Troy and get his son's MC back.

Last night he was supposed to collect four more men but they never showed up. They were supposed to bring the plans for the tunnel entrance. Without that, they had to depend on Breaker and he knew he couldn't trust that man any further than he could throw him. Jerry had told him it wasn't Deke who shot Bear but he did say it was Breaker.

Oscar's lips thinned. He had something special planned for Breaker but first he had to find his way inside the compound. That reminded him, he should give the men he had on watch a call and find out what they were doing to prepare for his upcoming visit. He had to know what was going on in Troy. The last thing he wanted was surprises, as he didn't take surprises well.

Reaching for his phone, he dialed the first number on his list. When the phone rang and rang and he got no answer, Oscar frowned. Hitting the second number, he got the same result. Growling, he hit the third number. When he got no response, he almost threw the phone on the ground. He began to pace while he thought about why his men weren't answering his calls.

He went over to the fire and began kicking dirt on the flames. His men began pitching a fit but Oscar growled back. "It's time to get some sleep. We need to push up the timeline. We need to get to Troy tomorrow and find out what the fuck in going on. And I don't need a bunch of drunks on my payroll."

"Speaking of payrolls," Creeper spoke up, "When do we get paid? We've been with you for a week now and we haven't gotten a dime for our effort."

Oscar wanted to hit the smartass. "I paid for your bikes, I bought the food you're eating and I pay for the gas to get this far. Until I can get to the money my son stashed, you'll just have to wait like the rest of them."

"And if that ain't good enough?" Creeper asked.

"Then collect your things and walk the fuck out of here. It's a long way home from here. I hope your boots can handle the walk," Oscar reminded him.

Creeper snorted. "Why should I walk when I got a bike?"

"Cuz that bike is mine. I bought it and if you choose to walk out before the job is done you don't get to walk away with it."

Creeper lazily got to his feet reaching behind him and grabbed the handgun he had stashed there. When he pulled it out in front of him, he never heard a second gun cocking in the background. The first he knew was when the echo of the shot sounded and a ripping pain stopped his heartbeat. Creeper's face paled and he fell to his knees. His life force was already gone by the time his body thumped to the dirt, releasing a small cloud of dust into the air.

Oscar didn't have to look at the shooter. Matty was sitting in the shadows and he would always have his back. Oscar looked around at the remaining men sitting there. "Anyone else have a problem with waiting to get paid?"

The men grumbled but didn't look him in the eyes. They might not say it but tonight's events didn't sit well with them. Creeper had only asked what everyone was thinking.

~*~

Back at the compound, Bane watched, as the men got ready. He was standing with Sarah.

Sarah snuggled in under his arm and softly asked, "What are you thinking?"

Bane sighed, exhaling a bit. "I used to do this same thing as these men and right now I was missing it."

Sarah felt her heartbeat speed up. She knew he had secrets but this sort of secret scared her. All too often, she saw the light in his eyes harden. His thoughts ran deep and often in the past, he would leave her alone and brood about his past. "Do you want your old life back?"

"Yes and no. I hated it for so long. Every day I met death and always cheated it, then on the day death came for me I was offered a choice. I took it and I don't regret it. I mean I've worked hard to get where I am but there's something still missing from the equation. A purpose. I need to believe in something again and while I've recovered, I've become restless thinking there must be more to life than what I'm living."

Sarah nodded. "I can understand that. Everyone needs something in their life, something to work for, to have passion for."

"Oh, and what was your passion?" Bane asked.

Sarah rolled her eyes. "My passion was staying alive. Looking over your shoulder twenty-four seven is no way to live. Being afraid every second of every day gets old after a while." She sighed. "I lived that life for fourteen years and would give it all up for just one place to live, one night of feeling safe, someone to protect me for even just a little while. I know when this threat is over, I still have to face Jack's brothers, and I'm hoping to find the courage to do that."

"If your brother doesn't stand beside you, I will be there for you," Bane assured her. "But I doubt your brother will turn his back on you, not now that he's found you again."

Sarah shrugged. "I haven't seen him in a long time. I grew up while he was gone. My life may not have turned out the way he wanted it but I think I've been on my own too long to get caught up in being his little sister again. I have to stand on my own two feet now. I just don't know any other way."

"Your brother doesn't look like the kind of man to let go so easily."

Sarah laughed out loud. "That's an understatement. He can be ruthless when he wants to be."

"Oh, of that I have no doubt. In charge of men his whole life. Protective of them and his family. He won't let go of you all that easy."

Priest walked over to them and stared at Bane for a long time. "You can't go back, you know that don't you?" he asked quietly.

Bane nodded. "I know but I can't go forward either. I watch them get ready for battle and I want to grab my rifle and follow them."

Priest nodded. "I know. I had to give up my past too. I'm not the man I once was either."

"But you did it for a woman, I didn't," Bane argued. He looked down at Sarah and smiled slightly. "I found my woman along the way, I can't deny that. But this isn't who I am. I know I need to forget my past but after living that life for so many years, I kind of miss it."

Priest stared at him for a moment then said, "Maybe when this is over you and I need to talk. I have an idea that might just work for both of us."

"When this is over," Bane echoed his statement.

Priest nodded.

~*~

Bane nodded back and their pact was sealed. Now all they had to do was get through this threat. Bane had avoided looking at Cricket and when he did, he found her watching him with a question in her eyes. He hadn't dared to get too close to her but he did watch her when she wasn't looking.

He looked around the room and caught sight of her, she was talking to her husband Raine, and her three children were sleeping in the corner of the clubhouse. He watched them with a hunger he didn't understand. Then he caught sight of Dusty sitting at a table eating a sandwich. He didn't understand the feelings he was experiencing just then, but he got some comfort in their presence.

When he looked over to the last place he saw Cricket he found her staring back at him and for some reason her stare unnerved him. He watched as she came toward him. He saw the determined look in her eyes and he almost smiled. She had a fire in her belly that reminded him of Grace.

He stood there and waited for her to join him. When she did, she had one question to ask, "Who are you?"

"My name is Theo Franks. But you knew that already didn't you?"

She nodded. "You remind me of someone I used to know, that's all."

Bane's eyes grew cold and he gave her a dead panned glare.

Cricket gasped and began to tremble. "No, it can't be," she whispered as she stumbled back. Raising her hand to her mouth, she repeated her statement, "This isn't possible." She turned and rushed away from him.

He turned back to Sarah and Priest.

Priest noticed Cricket's reaction and raised his eyebrow. "I think the cat's out of the bag, my friend."

Bane shrugged his shoulders. "She can't possibly know who I am."

"Maybe but are you willing to take the chance?"

"I don't have a choice do I?"

"Is that Cricket?" Sarah wondered.

"Yes, that's Cricket," Bane admitted. "And the young boy sitting at the head table is Dusty. The boy she raised."

~*~

Sarah glanced over at Dusty and gasped. He looked so much like Bane, the same jawline and the same curl to his hair. He would grow to be tall just like Bane as well. But his eyes were different. They were warm and full of life. She had to wonder just what kind of boy Bane had been. Then she saw a man who seemed to be the boy's father and she found Dusty also looked like him. The color of his hair, they also shared the same colored eyes and they also shared dimples.

She brushed her hand across her belly. That had been one dream she never dared to think about. A baby. Maybe if her life had been different, maybe if she wasn't being hunted. Too many maybes. Too many lost dreams.

Sarah looked over at the man who caught her interest. Bane told her his children were gone and while that was part of his past, she could never hope he would stick around long enough to be a part of her future. She was right now part of his present and that's all she could hope for. But she wouldn't give up her dreams.

Her childhood had been a nightmare but it was all she knew. Until he came along, she'd never trusted anyone to get close to her. She hadn't wanted anyone to get that close to her. Then she met him, now she dared to dream of a future...If they lived through the war that was breathing down their necks.

She glanced over at her brother and dared to hope again. Stone was the best at this sort of thing. She had heard his name whispered in the underground. Strangers knew more about him than she did and while that stung a bit, she'd always been proud of the man he'd become.

He led his men into battle and brought them home again. His men looked to him to find a way to win and they did. She had watched his return after his last deployment and when he got off the plane, she'd been so proud of him. She wanted to run out there and grab him but she couldn't. Instead, she blew him a kiss and disappeared into the crowd.

She couldn't visit her shame on him, he was a hero and she was anything but. Her eyes misted as she thought about the fact that he'd come all this way just to find her, to be here to protect her.

That meant something to her and it always would. Stone had told her just before Jack had forced him to leave that if she ever needed him he would be there for her. But when Jack died there was nothing he could do to protect her. He was fighting the war on terror in some far away land. Her life was over the moment she swung that bat. She wouldn't take him down with her. She got her mom to a safe place then she ran and she'd been running ever since that night.

Looking at Bane, she smiled. She had stopped running and found what she'd been looking for all this time. Looking around at the men and women here, she noticed something. Everyone here in this room was under a possible death sentence, yet they weren't afraid of it. The women were looking toward their men and their brotherhood to keep them safe and if they weren't safe, there was nowhere else they wanted to be but right beside the people that meant the most to them.

Sarah could feel that and now she knew why. Looking over at Bane again, she saw the light of life in his eyes. He wanted to live and that gave her hope. Then he looked over at her and smiled. The gentle smile shone in his eyes and all the way to his soul. But that look was strange to him and she didn't know why. His past? Maybe, but just maybe together, they could have a future, maybe together they could finally have peace.

Bane came over to her and took both her hands in his. Raising them to his mouth, he gently kissed her fingertips. "My dear, I don't want to leave you here all alone but you'll be with your brother if I don't make it back."

Sarah trembled at this. "What are you going to do? You're scaring me."

"I don't have time to explain everything right now but I'm going to follow Stone's men as a backup. They don't need me there but I have to be there. I have to do whatever I can to protect Cricket, Dusty and her children. I may never get the chance to meet them or watch them grow up but this is my chance to allow that to happen. If I make it back, you and I have a lot to discuss and we will discuss this I promise. As much as I'd like to stay out of this, I can't."

Sarah nodded slowly. "I know. I may not know everything, but this sort of thing is what you do best isn't it?"

"It used to be. I walked away from this life a year ago but this is not something I can walk away from."

Sarah let go of his hand and raised her hand to cup his whiskered jaw. Looking right into his eyes, she raised up on her tiptoes and pressed her lips to him. "Go, do what you have to do but you come back to me. Do you hear me? You come back to me."

Bane smiled slowly. Kissing her again, he assured her, "I will, and when I come back, you'll be mine forever."

Priest and James joined them and Priest knew the look in Bane's eyes. "You're going after them aren't you?"

Bane answered without saying a word.

James spoke up then, "So am I. It's not that I don't trust them but I want to be there with them."

Bane looked over at the other man and nodded. Then he shook his head. "I only wish I had my rifle. I left it behind a year ago at Stark's camp."

"Maybe you did but I didn't." James grinned. "It's in my trunk."

Bane smiled. "Let's go kick some ass."

Chapter Nine

Dressed in all black and wearing ski masks the six men from Pappy's group made their way noiselessly through the wooded area Oscar Buckley had chosen to wait for his men to arrive. It was three a.m. and the sliver of the moon didn't give them much light.

High in the treetops two men waited and watched the campground. The men with Buckley were asleep on the ground, snoring loudly and without a care in the world as they slept off the booze they'd drunk earlier in the night.

Buckley himself was sleeping away from both his men and the fire that was glowing more than burning. No one had banked it and within a short while, it would be out completely.

They searched the campsite for the girl and found her at last. One man split away from the group and made his way over to where she was laying.

It wasn't until he was practically on top of her that he noted the chains she was wearing. Buckley had chained her wrists and ankles to a tree. The man paused for a moment to find a solution and then he crept up to her. Carefully placing his hand over her mouth, she jerked awake. He leaned in close enough to whisper in her ear, "I'm not here to hurt you. We're here to rescue you. Do you understand?"

~*~

Amy nodded slowly. She looked around at the sleeping camp and began to shake. Then she saw the shadows moving around the camp and knew this man had others with him. Maybe they could get her away without anyone seeing them. Or before anyone else noticed she was gone.

"Don't move and don't rattle those fucking chains." The man took his hand away from her mouth and moved down to her feet. He was there only a moment before she felt the first chain fall away. A few minutes later, the second chain dropped away.

She groaned softly at the relief she felt. She turned her head to see the man who was offering her freedom and almost screamed a warning. Then she heard a thud and saw Matty crumble to the ground. He'd been raising his weapon to shoot the man helping her. From out of the darkness, a knife had been thrown and it struck Matty dead center in his chest. Matty didn't even have time to warn the others.

The man growled low and moved to her hands. Moments later, she was free of her shackles and the man scooped her up in his arms and moved her into the darkness surrounding the camp. Another shadow moved in as they were moving out.

The man carried her further away from camp before he stopped and laid her on the group. Assisting her to a sitting position, he asked her if she was all right.

Amy whispered, "I'm okay. Is my dad okay?"

The man nodded and removed his ski mask. Even in the dark, she knew she'd never see his face but at least this was better than nothing. She hated the ski mask.

"My mom? Did she make it?" Amy whispered hoarsely.

"Honey, I don't know. All I know is that your dad is waiting for you and we're here to help you get to him."

Amy looked over her shoulder at the direction of the camp. When she looked back she asked, "What about them?"

"Don't you worry about them."

"Okay," she whispered softly. "This kind of violence was new to her. She hadn't ever imagined it, not even in her worst nightmare.

"Come on baby girl, we got to go." He patted her on the leg and picked her up again.

Moving through the woods at an alarming speed, all Amy could do was hold on and pray he didn't trip.

Behind them, the sounds of gunshots were heard and still the man carried her away from the shooting. He broke through the woods into a clearing and they found several vehicles parked there. One man stood by the back of a SUV with a gun in his hands.

He opened the back of the vehicle and then carrying her, he put her inside. "Where are the others?" he asked.

"They should be right behind us," the man answered as he took stock of her injuries.

A few minutes later, four men broke out of the woods and joined them.

"Well? How did it go?" the man standing guard of the SUV asked.

"Oscar Buckley and three men got away but we took care of his numbers," one man told him.

Another man spoke up as well, "When the shooting started, Oscar jumped up and ran. He didn't raise his weapon or look after his own men, he turned yellow and ran off into the darkness. At least his men defended themselves."

"What about Matty Buckley?"

"That bastard was gonna shoot Rhymes in the back like the coward he was. Unfortunately, he met my blade. Then I got mad and shackled him to a tree. I left whoever is still alive a message." One of the men smiled and only the whites of his teeth showed in the darkness of the night around them.

"Let's get this show on the road." Turning to look at Amy he said, "We have a family reunion to attend."

Without saying another word, they all got into the vehicles and drove away.

~*~

Moments later, two more men exited the woods. They too, were dressed in black from head to toe. They walked over to another vehicle hidden from the rest. Each man broke down his own weapon silently, carefully packing it away in its own case. Neither man was in a hurry and they took the time they needed to secure everything down tight.

James finally glanced over at Bane. "I'm kind of glad our services weren't needed tonight."

Bane nodded. "Yeah, me too. It's been a while since I had to shoot my rifle."

"You know that's a mighty fine weapon."

Bane nodded. "I only got the very best. I had quite a collection at one time and I used them all."

James hesitated briefly, almost as if he wanted to say something. Then instead of saying anything, he closed the trunk and moved to the front of the vehicle. Getting behind the wheel while Bane got in the passenger seat he started the car and pointed it towards Troy.

~*~

Oscar Buckley wheezed as he ran through the woods on his way back to his camp. He'd stayed away long enough to make sure the camp would be empty of all hostiles. As he left the safety of the trees, the dawn had broken and there was enough light to see everything.

His men were laying crumpled on the ground, their eyes glazed over in death. He searched for his son's body and finally he saw Matty. He was chained to a tree, the same tree they had chained Breaker's little bitch to last night.

Matty's shirt was stained with red, now drying in the heat of another warm day. But it wasn't his shirt that drew Oscar's gaze, it was his eyes, blazing with fury. Someone had slapped duct tape over the boy's mouth so he couldn't shout out a warning. Oscar stomped over to his son and unlocked the handcuffs, then he tore the duct tape off Matty's mouth and listened to him scream as the tape ripped off more than it should have.

"What happened here?" Oscar motioned to his chest.

"I saw the man unlocking Amy's cuffs and I raised my gun to shoot him when out of nowhere a knife hit me in the chest. The blow caught me by surprise and I blacked out a moment. When I came to, I was cuffed to the tree and everyone else was dead. You were gone and I thought I was going to die here."

Oscar growled. "Those lousy bastards caught us off guard." Looking over at his son he asked, "Are you going to be able to ride?"

Matty shook his head. "I can try but I need medical attention first." He looked down and saw the open wound on his chest. "Damn that's a lot of blood. I may not be able to go anywhere for a while."

Oscar growled again. "I can't wait boy. We can get the wound stitched up and then we got to ride. This carnage needs to be paid for with their blood."

Matty turned his head when a branch snapped.

Oscar snapped his head around to see three men coming out of the woods and they were looking around the campsite in a daze.

"What the fuck happened?" one of the men asked.

"What the fuck do you think happened, you dumb ass?" Oscar got to his feet and approached them. "We were ambushed by the MC we were going after." He stomped closer to the three men standing there. "We almost died because you guys can't handle your drink. They got too close and not one of you heard them coming."

All three men glared back at him but not one of them said a word.

Oscar looked mad enough to just shoot them rather than take their guff. Oscar rubbed his hands along his jaw. Looking around the camp again, he shook his head. Then he turned to his son. Motioning toward Matty he ordered, "Grab him, we have to find someone to stitch him up so we can get to Troy. I want to watch that club burn to the ground."

"But boss," one of his men broke into the conversation. "Won't that burn the money as well?"

Oscar shook his head. "The money is in the tunnel, if Breaker doesn't open the tunnel it will be safe enough. We can look for it after the MC burns."

Two of the men went over to Matty and each man grabbed him under the arms.

Matty almost passed out when they got him upright. He swayed and tipped his head back.

One of the men holding him looked over at Oscar, "Err boss, I don't think Matty is going anywhere for a while."

Oscar growled out loud. He needed vengeance now, not when Matty felt better. "Let's get someone out here to stitch him up and maybe he'll be able to ride after that."

The lone man, Mikey disappeared and shortly after that, they heard the sound of a bike engine starting. The other two men lowered Matty to the ground and waited. Oscar looked around again and shook his head. "We need to get him out of here. Any one coming here will report the bodies and then we'll have the badges sticking their noses into our business." He walked over to the fire and began kicking dirt on it. "Let's move him closer to the parking lot."

They grabbed Matty and dragged him closer to the parking lot. Oscar went around and picked up the men's weapons then went through their pockets for anything that might help him. He opened their wallets and emptied them, pocketing their money.

Shaking his head, he followed his men leaving the dead behind. They could rot for all he cared. Oscar was so caught up in his darkness nothing mattered except what he wanted.

*

It was dawn when several vehicles drove into the parking lot of the compound. Doors opened as men and women poured out of the building and rushed forward to find out how the mission went.

One man pushed his way through the crowd and skidded to a stop fully just in back of the open door of the SUV.

Amy looked up and tears rolled down her face. "Daddy," she barely whispered.

Breaker heard her cry and knelt at her feet. "Baby, are you okay?" he asked as his eyes scoured her body. He saw the bruises and dried blood as well as the marks on her wrists and ankles from the handcuffs.

She nodded. "I am now daddy." She lunged for him.

Breaker gathered her small body in his arms. Tears ran down his face and he hugged her. "Oh baby girl, I'm so sorry. I'm sorry."

Amy hugged him tight and couldn't speak. Her nightmare might be over but she knew this situation wasn't finished. It wouldn't be until Oscar Buckley was dead.

Breaker lifted his daughter and carried her into the clubhouse where Raine was waiting to look her over for injuries. He took her to a bedroom down the hall from the main room. Amy looked embarrassed when Raine began removing her dirty ragged clothing. Breaker turned his back but wouldn't leave the room.

Cricket joined him and together, they assessed Amy's injuries. When Raine was finished, he went to stand by Breaker while Cricket helped Amy to the bathroom.

Breaker turned his head and asked, "How bad was it?"

Raine shook his head. "They weren't gentle with her but for the most part she's intact. They didn't molest her fully but they cuffed her. She must have fought them at some point but they were bigger and stronger than she is."

"Is she gonna be ok?" Breaker dared to ask.

"She will be unless you turn your back on her," Raine told him squarely.

Breaker snarled, "That ain't gonna happen brother. She's my whole world. I'll never turn away from my baby girl."

Raine smiled. "That's good to hear." Slapping him on the back he suggested, "Why don't we go find out what happened tonight? Cricket will help your daughter and bring her out when she's ready."

Breaker ran his fingers over the top of his head and nodded. "Yeah, I want to hear what happened."

When they left, they walked down the hall to the main room.

One of the men on the mission was making his report, "When we got there we did recon and found Buckley's group. The fire was mostly out and everyone was sound asleep. He had no guards posted and the men were sleeping off whatever they had drank hours before. We saw about a half a dozen liquor bottles all over the camp." He looked over at Pappy. "They were all empty. There were also drag marks leading off into the woods. I followed the tracks and found one of his men with a hole in his head." Shaking his head he also said, "We don't know what happened or why but it looks like Oscar Buckley shot his own man."

"He didn't," Amy told them from behind.

Everyone turned and watched silently as she walked over to her father. She had showered and was wearing fresh clothes. Her long hair hung to her shoulders in wet rings. She limped as she crossed the floor to her father.

When his arm came around her shoulders, Amy looked over at Deke and Pappy. "It wasn't Oscar who shot that man, it was Matty. Creeper was drunk and looking for a paycheck from Oscar and Oscar told him he had to wait until they got the money that was hidden here. Creeper didn't like that idea and Oscar said he hoped he enjoyed the walk home because if he left, he'd be on foot. Oscar told him he paid for the bike, food and gas. Then Creeper stood up like he was going to pull his gun out and Matty shot him in the back." Shaking her head, she moved closer to her dad and sobbed. "He didn't even give the man a chance. He just shot him."

No one said a word as they thought about what she said. Then Deke looked over at her and asked, "Did they talk about the plans to get inside the compound or anything else while you were with them?"

Amy turned haunted eyes to Deke and the others. "They said that if my dad didn't follow through and do what he was supposed to, he'd kill me right in front of him. Then he'd firebomb the entire compound. Oscar said he'd get in one way or the other." She shook her head. "Then he said he'd keep you alive long enough to hang you upside down and skin you while you were still breathing. He wanted to show everyone who came to avenge your demise what he does with traitors to his family. He bragged that he and Matty would be kings with direct access to the cartels and the drug lords, they were gonna rule the whole east coast."

Deke stared at the little girl and shook his head. Moving closer he squatted down to her level. Taking her hand, he kissed her fingers. "Little girl, I'm sorry you had to go through that but I promise you Oscar Buckley and Matty will not survive the war they're bringing to us. We won't give up or give in to their demands, nor will I willingly lose a man, woman or child to him. Oscar only thinks he's tough but us?" He looked around the clubhouse. "We're tougher than he will ever be. We will survive and show Oscar Buckley to the gates of hell."

"Do you promise?" Amy whispered the words.

Deke leaned forward and brushed his lips on her forehead. "That's more than a promise, that's a vow and I don't give them lightly."

Chapter Ten

Bane stood by the window overlooking the backyard. He seemed calm and collected but inside, he was writhing and the rage he hadn't felt in so long was winning the battle to break loose.

Sarah came up behind him wrapping her arms around his waist. Laying her face on his back, she breathed in his scent. It wasn't the same today as it had been yesterday or even last night. Today there was a tang to it. A sharp tang that if she could taste it she knew it would burn her tongue. Sarah began to tremble. Her arms withdrew slowly and she stepped away.

But before she could take more than one small step away Bane began speaking in a low voice, "Please don't...don't leave me. Can I tell you a secret?"

Sarah stopped and looked at his back. She swallowed hard and whispered, "Of course. You can tell me anything."

Bane kept his gaze on the backyard as he spoke, "I've lived my entire life watching people. I never understood the compassion people had for one another. I never felt the need to. I suppose that link was missing from my soul and before a year ago, I never missed it. Then I did the only decent thing in my miserable life. I tried to stop a man hell bent on destroying this place. I destroyed the man and his army. At the last minute, he got off a shot that would have ended my life but instead, I got a second chance. I put the past behind me and tried to let it go, then this came up. My past just won't leave me alone and I'm not sure that I want it to. I thought I could start over but even when I try, the past just sucks me back in." He turned and looked at her. His eyes glistened in the shadows. "But one thing I do control is who I'm with. I want you woman, I want you more than life itself, but I can't force you to stay with me. I did that once and I will not do it again."

Sarah stared at him and listened as she trembled a little.

"I took a woman once and I thought I loved her, but she didn't love me. Yet, I couldn't no... I wouldn't let her go. I forced her to stay with me and back then, I wasn't a nice man. You could almost say I was brutal to her. Oh, I never hurt her, but I wouldn't let her tell me no either. I hurt that woman so much, yet she found her small piece of heaven with another man, my brother."

Sarah gasped but kept her thoughts to herself.

Bane continued with his story, "I couldn't let that go so I searched for them for a number of years. I was ready to crush them both and grind their bones under my heel, instead I found Cricket. My Grace and my brother Orrin were gone, as was the daughter I never knew I had. Cricket reminded me so much of her mother I couldn't stand it. I decided to test her just to see what she was made of. It didn't really surprise me to find that she had enough spunk inside her to handle just about anything I asked of her. She told me one time that she didn't have a choice before, that someone else dictated what kind of life she led but that wasn't the way she wanted it. No she was as straight as an arrow and she showed me real honor, she held her ground even when the ground beneath her was crumbling." He shook his head as if he still felt baffled by this.

Sarah stood quietly almost afraid to speak in case he stopped talking, as he'd never shared so much with her before.

"That's what made me take Priest's offer for a do over that night. I should have died but I didn't. It was almost as if the do over gave me a new chance to change my ways. I wanted a new start so bad. I found my peace when I asked Grace and Orrin for their forgiveness that night. I also vowed to change and I think I could still do that." He paused and looked around at the little room. "Then this came up and I found myself falling back into the same kind of life I so wanted to forget. But this is what I'm good at, these are the skills I have that no one else has to equal me. Somewhere along the line, I forgot that part of the equation.

Now I have to take a stand and I'm afraid if I do I may not come back to the man I was becoming. I'll be stuck with the man I was."

"I know all about hiding and changing my life," Sarah told him. "I wish someone had offered me a do over twelve years ago. Although, I doubt I would take it. Jack Connors deserved what happened to him. If I hadn't stepped up, both my mom and I would be dead and no one would know the truth about what kind of man he really was. He hid behind his family's name and everything it stood for all his life. His brothers and father are just as bad. They are all two faced and I have no doubt that when and if they find me, they will kill me."

"The hell they will." Bane growled as he turned to face her. "I'm sure between your brother and I, the Connors don't stand a chance. If they want a war, they've come to the right place. I'll give them a war they never thought of. Your brother may have to follow the law but I don't. They won't see the kill shot I deliver but they'll feel it. I'll make them bleed."

Sarah shuddered but she believed him. She saw him pause then he leaned toward her and pressed his lips on hers. The kiss deepened and before she knew it, he had picked her up and pressed her against the wall. He opened her up with a kiss and pressed his hard cock into her wet core. "I want you so bad right now."

"I know," she whispered as his lips trailed down her neck to her collarbone. When his lips stopped over her artery and he could feel her heart racing she groaned. "I want you too."

Bane slipped his hand down her pants and into her underwear. Her bare skin was warm and when he touched her nether lips, he found them wet and slick. Pressing deeper, he slid his way home and deepened his touch.

Sarah groaned and opened her legs. Bane nipped her neck and slid his fingers deeper inside her. His thumb found her clit and thumbed it. He could feel her body begin to shimmer and shake, as she got closer to exploding. Bane felt his own body harden. He wanted to find his own release but she deserved this moment. This time was for her and he wouldn't deny her.

Instead, he worked all the harder to get her where she wanted to be. His strokes were harder and faster as his fingers worked her better than he had ever before done with a woman and soon she was there. She threw her head back and he quickly covered her mouth with his hand. He couldn't allow her to scream her release here in the clubhouse. Anyone could barge in on them and this wasn't for everyone to see. The only one he wanted to witness her release was him.

Bane let her go but pressed his lips on hers and drank her sweetness. "I could do this every single day for the rest of my life," he whispered.

"Me too." She hesitated then whispered, "I know you may not want to hear this and you may not believe it but I think I love you."

Bane smiled and looked down at her, "You only *think* you love me? Does that mean you don't know for sure? Because I know for sure. I do love you. I thought I knew what love was but I didn't really. I never had feelings like everyone else, but this between us? I think that's love."

Sarah looked him in the eyes. "I do love you. I just wasn't sure you would want my love."

"But I do want it. I will keep it safe right there in my heart. I can't take away your past pain but I will protect you until the day I die from ever having any more. But first we have to make it through the war Oscar Buckley is waging on not only us but everyone here."

He rested his forehead against her and agreed with her. "Maybe we can use what Amy learned to stop him cold. We demolished his numbers enough he can't come straight on, but knowing that man, he's got plan B up his sleeve. We just have to think of what that is and stop it."

Sarah pressed her mouth on his and before the kiss got out of hand she slipped from his grasp. "Come on, let's go find the others and see what they've got planned." She smiled gently at him. "I want the rest of my life with you and that isn't going to happen until this is over, one way or the other."

Bane nodded. "Come on, let's win this war."

~*~

As night grew closer, the men were talking over the situation and not coming up with any kind of solution. Tempers were growing to the peak and they needed something to break the tension.

"Come on guys, we need to come up with a plan of action. Hopefully, before Buckley gets to our front door." Deke growled.

"What was it Amy said, if Breaker didn't open the tunnel he'd firebomb the clubhouse and burn it to the ground?" Pappy repeated. "Since he's down on man power he might do that just to be safe. He can't count on Breaker anymore, so he might not have a choice."

"So, all we have to do is get our best men in the woods to watch for him and take him out before he gets close," Mountain suggested.

"And what if he's out there watching us? Waiting for us to lower our guard already?" Bane suggested.

"What do you think we should do?" Deke argued snidely. "Since you seem to shoot down every idea we've had so far. What do you think we should do?"

"I've been looking around, studying the area and I think I found a way around this. Now Pappy's men are good but the less people out there the better."

Deke sat up and leaned forward. "What did you have in mind, old man?"

Bane gritted his teeth at the mention of his age. He didn't want Pappy to think he was too old for his much younger sister but he could overlook the snide remark in this case. "I think James, myself and two of Pappy's best should sneak out after dark and find a position we can watch from. You can get your men in position within your gates but I think the four of us have a better chance to get to him out there. He might think we're ready inside the fence but he might not expect us to be out there too."

Pappy stared at him for a moment while he thought about the suggestion. Turning to Dkee he asked, "Could that work? With only four men?"

One of Pappy's men cleared his throat. "Pappy, remember we got most of his men last night. He's only got three, maybe four men left and that includes Oscar himself. I don't know if Matty made it or not. That knife cut him deep but whatever, he doesn't have that many men left. He can't come at us head on." Pausing, he added, "The old man's plan might just work."

Bane gritted his teeth. While he was considerably older than they were he didn't like to be reminded about it.

Deke glanced over at the cot Gator was resting on. He still hadn't come around from being shot yesterday and until they neutralized this threat, they couldn't get him proper medical help. Reva was going nuts worrying about him and Deke was growing anxious as well. He couldn't bear the thought of losing his best friend.

He got up and walked slowly to the window overlooking the dooryard. He noticed Reva walking out to the gate to wait for the bus bringing her adopted kids home from school. Today would be their last day of public school until this threat was over. They all wanted to go today for some program for their class projects or some dumb shit like that. Deke thought they would be all right as Oscar Buckley had still been in Palmer this morning. Now, he wasn't so sure.

His gut twisted as he saw the bus pull up to the gate. Benny, Jack and Alaina got off and as the bus pulled away a man stepped out of the woods and grabbed Benny.

Reva stopped in her tracks. She didn't scream or run to the others but instead she waited just inside the gates. Jack and Alaina hurried to get to safety but turned and watched as their brother struggled against the man holding him.

Then the man called out to Reva. She pushed the two children behind her and slowly walked toward the man holding Benny.

Suddenly, there was a gun in his hand and he had it pointed at Benny's head.

Reva shook as she continued to walk forward. When she got near enough the man pushed Benny down into the dirt and grabbed Reva.

Then he turned and raised his weapon. Firing a bullet into the air, they all heard Alaina scream.

Everyone rushed to the front door and out into the dooryard. Aliana, Benny and Jack rushed to stand behind the men. The man holding Reva called out to them. "Hold up. I won't hesitate to kill this woman. I'm here to make a deal. I'm with Oscar Buckley and he only wants the man who murdered his son Bear to come forward. He wants Deke Tory. Are you there Deke? Are you man enough to face him?" The man smiled evilly. "Because he sure wants to meet you. He says he's got a bullet with your fucking name on it."

Deke stepped out of the protection of his men. "Let Reva go and I'll meet him face to face."

The man grinned. "Are you fucking nuts man? I let her go and your men will kill me. No, this little lady is coming with me. Her and me are gonna have a little fun if you know what I mean. Oscar said he'll be here tomorrow to deal with you and your MC."

Reva struggled then screamed in pain when the man holding her wrenched her tighter to him. He grabbed her hair and pulled it to get her to behave. Reva looked over the yard at Deke with tears in her eyes. "Deke you take care of my Gator and tell him that I love him. If he ever wakes up, you tell him that okay?"

"Aww, ain't that sweet?" The man gripped her tighter. "Yeah Deke, you tell her man she loves him and that she'll die lovin' him." He laughed and began backing up into the woods again dragging Reva with him.

Every man standing there helpless listened as a moment later they all heard Reva scream. But then they all heard her scream get cut off and the silence that followed was overwhelming.

Deke turned to his men and shouted, "Fucking hell!" Then he remembered there were children present and he glanced at them. All three were huddled together. They looked scared to death. All three were sobbing as Benny had blood and dirt running down his face from when the man had thrown him to the ground.

Mountain, Sam and Wiley each grabbed one of the kids and hauled them inside the clubhouse. Once there, Cassie took over and had them sit down at one of the tables when she cleaned Benny's face with a wet cloth. Peaches and Sarah were there as well.

When the men entered the room, Deke looked over at Bane and growled. "Can you fucking track that bastard? Can you find him and find us a way to get Reva back before they kill her?"

Bane nodded. "I'll make him wish he'd never been born."

"Do it." Deke growled harshly. "Do it quick and I don't care how clean. I can't have Gator waking up to find out his woman got taken and killed while he was sleeping. He'd kill me if I had to tell him that."

"Uncle Deke," Benny called out.

Deke rushed over to the children and bent down on one knee in front of the boy.

"I'm sorry Uncle Deke," Benny choked out.

"Sorry? What are you sorry for?" Deke asked.

"I'm sorry mom got taken. If I hadn't been so slow getting off the bus we would have been behind the gate before he could grab me." Benny sobbed. "Now, he's got Mom and he's gonna hurt her."

Deke's heart broke as he listened to their sobs. He gathered Benny into his hug and told him, "Now don't you fuss. I'll get your mom back for you. Theo is going out to look for her and he'll find out where they have her and we'll rescue her, don't you worry about that." He looked at all three kids. "We'll get her back. I promise."

Alaina shook her head. "Please don't make promises you might not be able to keep. That man wants you dead. He might hurt our mom to get that wish. All our lives, people had made us promises they never intended to keep. Reva and Gator have been the only ones who have kept their promises." She looked over at Gator laying so still on the cot next to the wall. "Gator might die and now Reva's gone too. We may not have a family anymore, so don't you make a promise you can get her back without making that true."

"Oh sweet girl…" Cassie bent down to hug her. "You have a family here with us. We're all your family, don't you know that? Reva and Gator adopted you but all three of you belong to all of us."

Alaina burst into tears and hugged Cassie tight. "You swear? You really swear?"

"You bet your booties I swear," Cassie whispered. "You guys belong to us."

~*~

Bane turned and walked down the hall to his bedroom.

James followed, stopping off at his own room briefly but he and Priest joined Bane.

As he closed the door behind himself, Priest looked over at Bane. "Can you track them?"

Bane glared at them. "Yeah, I can track the fucker."

"Then what's the problem?" Priest asked.

"I'm not prepared!" Bane yelled at the other man. "A year ago I had the equipment I knew and was familiar with. And now I don't have that edge."

Priest glanced over at James and nodded.

James stepped forward and laid what looked like a bag on the bed.

Opening the bag, Bane pushed him out of the way. He searched the bag like an old friend. He should, this was his bag, his to go kit.

Reverently, he spread the roll out and there in front of him were the tools of his former trade. Each tool had its own place and was neatly tucked into said place His scopes were present, his blades were tucked into their own slots and his three handguns ordered and built just for his hand by a master gunsmith were present.

This was by no means all his tools of the trade but it was a beginning. With this stuff, he was comfortable and it felt like he was welcoming an old friend to have them back in his hands. Then he searched his equipment in the roll but didn't see what he needed. His mini crossbow wasn't there.

Looking over at Priest he asked, "You didn't happen to grab my rifle or mini crossbow did you?"

Priest nodded and glanced over at James. The other man disappeared and returned a few minutes later with both pieces.

Bane grabbed the cross bow and looked it over in detail. His hand slid down the trigger and fitted the butt into his shoulder. It fit perfectly.

While James had been gone, Bane had changed his attire and now dressed in black he attached the small crossbow to the heavy leather belt he wore. Fitting a handgun to the cross-back holster he wore, he also fitted a pair of blades to his belt. The last thing he did was slip a dark cap over his head. Completely hiding the grey in his hair.

Walking over the window, he opened it and slipped outside. Before he turned to close the window, he told Priest, "You tell Deke to be ready for anything tonight. I'll find Reva and keep her with me but that means men are going to die by my hand. I guess there really are no do overs in life are there?"

"That depends on what you do when this is over, my friend," Priest replied. "We'll talk when you get back. Be safe and watch your back."

Bane looked over at James. "Are you going to be out there in the shadows?"

James nodded.

"Be careful, we're hunting a mad man tonight. One that had absolutely no fear of death."

"Agreed. He's out for revenge, but revenge over what act? He doesn't even know yet." James nodded. "He isn't going to like the fact his oldest son betrayed the trust he gave him. He isn't going to believe until he sees the evidence with his own eyes and even then, he won't let it go."

Bane shrugged. "Then we show him the way to hell and push him into the gates ourselves don't we?" He looked over at Priest. "If I don't make it back, you watch over Sarah for me. Don't let those bastard Connor brothers get near her. Don't you let them touch her with their filth."

Priest's eyes grew cold. "They won't touch a hair on her head."

He nodded then turned and disappeared in the growing shadows of the late afternoon.

~*~

Priest and James turned and went back to the main room.

Deke, Sam, Iceman, Mountain and everyone there watched as two men joined them, even Pappy's men were watching them.

Finally, Deke asked, "Where is your friend?"

"He went hunting," Priest told them.

Pappy moved to stand in front of Priest. "He went alone?" he asked softly.

Priest looked over at the other man. They knew each other now and without saying too much, Priest nodded. "He went alone."

Pappy knew Priest would never put anyone here in danger but he didn't know Theo that well. He'd heard Priest speak of him and he knew Priest had been gone a while making contact with the other man but he'd never met him until he'd seen Sadie with him. He seemed so much older than his sister and while he wasn't used to playing big brother he wanted his sister to be happy. He couldn't say a word about her being with an older man. His own McKenna was so much younger than he was. And their relationship was working.

"So now what?" Deke growled.

Pappy turned to him and said simply, "Now we wait."

"I can't just fucking sit here and wait," Deke grumbled and he ran his fingers through his hair.

Pappy grabbed him by the bicep and hauled him closer. "If Priest said we wait, then we wait. He trusts his man Theo and that means we have to trust him as well. Or we could go out there on our own and risk everything."

Deke gazed into Pappy's eyes and saw nothing but conviction in them. He nodded and pulled his arm out of Pappy's grasp. He turned to his men and saw the expression on their faces. Then he looked over at Cassie and asked her, "Can you get the kids out of here? If they come in here shooting, I don't want the kids getting caught in the crossfire."

Cassie and the other women began gathering the children together and moving them down the hall. They had built an underground shelter beyond the basement walls for storms in the past year or so and that's where they took the children.

Cricket broke away from the group and approached Priest. Looking into his eyes she had to ask, "Is Theo going to be okay out there on his own?"

Priest hesitated then nodded. 'He'll be okay."

Shaking her head she said, "I don't know why but he reminds me of a man I once knew. But that's impossible, Bane died a year ago. He died while saving not only my life but the lives of everyone who calls this place home."

"Maybe he had something to prove to you. Maybe he wanted to know if he had the same kind of honor you did. Maybe he found what he was finally looking for." Priest watched her face.

Cricket gasped softly. She reached out and gripped his arm. "You tell him that I care about what happens to him, despite what my mother did to him. He deserves a good life and a good woman. He didn't have that with her but he could with his Sarah. Tell him I wish him well."

Priest waited for a moment then nodded. "I'll tell him."

He watched her walk away and he knew that she knew who Theo was. He only hoped she would protect his secret. That with her silence, she would give him a second chance to have his do over in spite of this lapse.

After about two hours of waiting, James grabbed his phone and searched his text messages. He grinned slightly then moved over to where Priest was standing with Deke and Pappy. He showed them the text without saying a word. The text read, *"One down four to go. Reva still alive."*

They all turned as they heard Gator's weakened voice call out, "Deke, what the fuck is going on?" His voice was barely more than a whisper.

Deke turned toward his friend and saw the other man's eyes were open. His skin still looked pale and a little on the grey side. His face was drawn in pain and his eyes were narrowed as he stared at Deke and the others.

Deke rushed over to him and knelt down on one knee.

"What the everlovin hell hit me?" Gator asked. "A fucking Mac truck?"

Deke snorted. "Try a high powered bullet."

Gator's eyes widened. "Reva and the kids? Are they all right?" He tried to sit up but didn't make it. He groaned and flopped back down on the cot. He grabbed Deke's shirt and garbled, "Is my family alright?"

"The kids are safe man, I swear," Deke told him.

Gator focused his eyes and narrowed them as Deke's words sank in. "And Reva?"

"Reva is in a little trouble right now but we're working on it."

Gator thought about his word then snarled, "You're working on it? What the fuck does that mean, you're working on it?" He tried to sit up again, but he couldn't pull himself up. "You'd better tell me what's going on here man or I'm going to beat the shit out of you."

Deke pressed Gator's shoulder back to the mattress and held him down. "I need you to listen to me. Listen carefully and relax. Oscar Buckley is outside the gates somewhere. He got one of his men to grab Reva and he's holding her hostage. He wants the man who killed Bear and he wants me. We got him down to three or four men and he's a desperate man."

"Then why are we sitting on our hands here?" Gator looked around and saw the number of men. "Why is everyone still here? Why aren't you out there looking for her?"

"We are looking for her," Deke assured his friend and VP.

"Fucking hell!" Gator swore with draining strength. "I can't lose her man. She's my whole world and has been for longer than I can remember."

Deke grabbed the other man's shoulder. "We'll get her back. We have the best out there searching for her. He just texted us that she is still alive. He'll bring her back to you."

"He?" Gator snarled. "You got one man out there looking for her. One man against five fuckin murderers?"

"He's the best there is man," Deke assured his friend. "You have to trust me on this one."

"I do trust you man," Gator admitted. "You haven't let me down in almost twenty years. I do trust you. Just bring her back to me. I can't live without that woman. I wouldn't even want to try."

James' phone pinged again and the sound rang loudly in the silent room. James read the message and held up two fingers. Then he smiled tightly and hand pumped his fist.

~*~

Bane stepped carefully through the wooded area behind the compound. He found the first man leaning against a tree. In his hand was a shotgun and he was staring at the buildings not too far away. He was smoking a cigarette and had no idea Bane was standing behind him.

Bane reached down at his belt and silently took one of his knives out. Taking careful aim, he slid the steel into the back of the man's neck slicing through his brainstem.

The man never got the chance to say a word as he slid first to his knees then to faceplant in the dirt. No sound was heard by anyone nearby as death took him. He most likely never even knew he was about to die.

Bane left him where he dropped and moved on. Deeper in the woods, he thought he heard a sound. He moved in that direction and found himself outside a small camp. They had no fire but there was a camp light sitting on a stump.

There was one man sitting there staring at the woman he'd kidnapped.

Reva sat there with her hands bound behind her back. She wasn't crying or scared but Bane noticed she wore fresh bruises on her face and her shirt was torn. There was a cloth around her mouth tied tightly behind her head.

There was another body there, laying against the tree. Bane could see he was wounded. His shirt was stained with dry blood and he had a feeling this was Matty Buckley. The men who raided the camp in Palmer reported Matty had been badly wounded.

That meant there would be two other men, maybe three counting Oscar Buckley himself. Bane grabbed his crossbow and loaded the small bolt. Taking aim, he could only hope Reva wouldn't scream when he killed the man sitting next to her.

Letting loose the bolt it hit dead on.

The man flopped over backward without saying a word or letting any sound loose.

Reva didn't scream, in fact she didn't even look surprised at what happened. Instead, she slowly turned her head and stared out into the woods searching for the assailant.

Bane walked into the camp area and instead of walking to free her, he went over to where Matty was laying.

Matty didn't even roust when Bane knelt beside him. His eyes were closed and Bane could see the artery in his neck was barely beating. Bane pushed open his shirt and saw the knife wound was barely stitched. The stitches were uneven and poorly put in. Matty's skin was cooling and grey. Bane knew with one look that Matty wouldn't be long for this world. To end his suffering Bane raised his knife and cut the vein barely beating. He watched as the vein pumped fresh blood out and finally the blood slowed to a trickle and then stopped altogether.

He got to his feet and turned to Reva. "Are you all right?" he whispered.

Reva never said a word but nodded slowly instead. She watched him closely. Seeing every move he made carefully and precise. The gag had stopped her from making any sound but even when the man next to her died a violent death, she hadn't called out in any way.

Bane raised his blade again and cut through the gag in her mouth.

Reva didn't move until she felt the tightness let go. She spit out the cloth and waited.

Bane cut through the binding on her wrist.

Reva hissed as the pain rushed through her body but she didn't make any other sound.

Bane reached down and helped her to her feet. Then he motioned her to follow him. Putting his finger to his mouth, he motioned for her to be quiet.

She nodded and followed him back into the woods.

He looked over his shoulder and mouthed the words, "How many left?"

Reva held up two fingers.

Bane nodded and searched the woods for the next man. It took him twenty minutes moving slowly and carefully through the woods to find him. He motioned for Reva to stay where she was and not to make a sound.

Reva did as she was told.

Bane moved closer. He grabbed both knives in his hands and stepped up behind the other man. Moving swiftly, he crossed the blades and brought them around the man's head. Quickly, efficiently, deadly he sliced through the other man's neck and pulled back.

The man barely had time to know he was in danger before he was dead. His head separated from the rest of his body before it thumped to the ground. Blood poured from the severing and spread out in front of him.

Bane stepped back and saw the look of horror on Reva's face.

She had raised her hands to cover her mouth but she didn't say anything.

Bane stepped closer and brought her head to the crook of her neck. "Hang on girl. Don't lose your shit yet. We still have one more man to find and he may be the worst."

Reva shuddered in his arms but she kept her quiet. She stepped away and nodded. She moved away completely and couldn't look him in the face.

Bane sighed deeply and stepped away. He hated this part of his job. Usually, he got satisfaction from witnessing the fear of people's faces but this fear was different. Although he would never harm her, she no longer trusted him and that bothered him. Odd, that he never had this feeling before either.

He moved closer to the compound and when they got as close as they could without reaching the fence line then he suddenly without warning dragged Reva to her knees. His hand covered her mouth before she could utter a sound. She didn't see anything out of order but she trusted him just enough to follow his lead.

They sat there and waited. Each second they waited seemed like an eternity.

Finally, Reva saw what Bane had seen a few minutes earlier.

Oscar Buckley stepped out of the shadows. He'd been moving closer to the compound all this time. In his hand was a bottle of what smelled like gasoline.

Reva's nose wrinkled when the scent finally hit her.

Bane turned to frown at her and when he shook his head, she got the message he was trying to get through to her.

She nodded and they both turned to where Oscar stood.

He glared at the compound on the other side of the fence. He had a cigar in his mouth and they both watched as the glowing end rolled with his movements.

Looking toward the main building, Bane couldn't see any movement coming from inside. The windows were dark and it looked like no one was there at all.

Then Oscar began mumbling to himself. They both listened to the other man's words and Bane's soul felt cold at his words.

"Fuckin cowards, that's what they are. They'd let one of their own women die rather than face up to the truth," Oscar ranted. "They brought this war on themselves. They killed my boy. Hell, they killed both my sons. They murdered my crew and now I have nothing left. For all I know, they spent the money I left with Bear and now I have nothing." he began to pace back and forth. He twisted and turned the bottle in his hands.

Bane watched as the rage inside the man took over. He understood that kind of rage. He'd often felt it himself. When he saw Oscar stop his pacing and turn to face the compound, he knew exactly what the man was going to do. He watched in horror as Oscar flipped the lighter open in and his thumb struck the wheel that flicked the flame. He saw the rag sticking out of the top of the bottle burst into flame and as Oscar lifted his hand to throw the flaming cocktail over the fence a shot rang out and Oscar staggered back dropping the bottle to the ground.

The bottle burst and the scent of gasoline spread quickly and burned everything it touched. It engulfed Oscar's body and soon his clothing caught fire.

Bane grabbed the back of Reva's head and brought it to his chest, so she wouldn't witness the other man burn to death.

Reva sobbed as she was pressed into his body. She didn't want to see what was going on a few feet away from where they sat.

He screamed as he tried to roll the fire out but the gas burned too quickly.

All they could hear was Oscar screaming. Finally, the screams stopped and the flames burned brightly.

Bane got up to his feet and hauled her away from the fire. He stumbled closer to the fence. Walking along the chain link fence they made their way to the front gate.

Men poured out of the clubhouse as they reached the front gate. Wiley pushed the buttons and the gate opened.

Bane walked Reva inside and she was immediately taken from him. She was hustled inside the clubhouse and Bane was left to answer questions.

"What the hell happened out there?" Deke growled.

"I took the first man out then found their camp. Reva and another man were there and so was Matty. Matty was almost dead but I made sure he was before we left. Then I found the second man and sent him to hell." He looked back at the burning embers of what was left of Oscar. "I have no clue who fired the shot there but he was the last one."

Just then, James walked out of the woods with a rifle in his hands. No one said a word as he moved past the group and disappeared into the clubhouse.

Slowly, everyone turned and followed him into the clubhouse.

Reva was next to her man, Gator and she was in his arms sobbing in relief since he was awake. Gator was holding her in an embrace that said he wasn't letting her go any time soon.

When Bane walked past them, Gator reached out his hand.

Bane paused before he took it. Looking Gator in the eyes, he heard the other man whisper, "Thank you for bringing my life back to me."

Bane nodded but didn't say anything. Instead, he let go and headed down the hall to the bedroom he claimed as his own. Opening the door, he saw Sarah sitting on the bed waiting for him. He saw the tears rolling down her face and the sight broke his heart.

He went over to her and knelt on the floor in front of her. She raised shaky hands and cupped both sides of his face. "I'm so glad you came back to me." She pushed the tight knit cap off his head.

"I'll always come back to you," he told her as he buried his face in her belly. He wrapped his arms around her waist and held her tightly for a moment.

Sarah ran her fingers through his hair. Her eyes were blurry from the tears she couldn't stop. "I love you. I don't care about your past, only the future. I want to stay right here beside you."

"Then I guess I don't have to beg you to stay with me huh?" He smiled slightly. "Are you sure about this? I'm not an easy man to live with. I'm so much older than you are and pretty much set in my ways. I can be incredibly demanding and stubborn to a fault but if you stay, I can try to change."

Sarah shook her head. "I don't want you to change just for me. If you change, I want it to be for our future. I love you just the way you are. As scary as that man can be, I don't want to change him. That's the man I fell in love with, that's the man I want you to be."

Bane smiled. "I can do that." His smile slid off his face and he looked at her intently. "But to start our life together, you need to know the whole truth about my past. Once you know the truth you may decide to go home with your brother."

Sarah waited for him to speak. She looked deeply into his eyes with confidence and didn't look away from him.

"My past includes being a hitman for most of my adult life. I killed people for a living and made more money than I will ever spend in three lifetimes. I was a cold, brutal man and I never thought I could change that. Then in the end, I learned forgiveness. I couldn't understand what Cricket was all about when she stood up to me, when she stood there with her head raised and told me she wasn't going to run. I learned what honor really was when she put her life on the line for every man, woman and child who lived here. Everything I knew as fact faded into nothing when I saw what she meant to these people. What she was beginning to mean to me. I saw the light of her mother's soul in her eyes and I saw something my brother told me years ago."

"What was that?" Sarah asked softly.

"Orrin told me there was more to life than simply getting by. He told me that to experience what life really meant I had to see it through someone else's eyes. The night I was shot, I did finally understand what he meant. I fully expected to die that night then Priest stepped out and offered me a do over." He closed his eyes and whispered, "I got my chance to change my life and today, my past sucked me back in. I guess I'm one that doesn't get a do over. I only hope you can live with the man I am becoming again."

Sarah cupped his face and leaned toward him. "Bane, I love you and that love means the world to me. I've been living on my own for more years than I care to remember. I lived in fear every single day and with you, I can forget that fear. You've given me that you took the fear away that was paralyzing my every waking moment. I know with you beside me, I no longer have to fear anything, even the Connor brothers."

He shook his head. "There's more. My real name is—"

She held up her hand and covered his mouth. "There is nothing in your past that will make me run from you. Nothing more that I need to know. You have a past the same as I do. And that's ok with me. I won't hold anything in your past against you. I fell in love with you, not your past."

Bane kissed the fingers she held over his mouth. "I have no clue where I'm going from here but I would consider it an honor if you would come with me."

"I will follow you to the ends of the earth," Sarah assured him. Then she leaned forward and pressed her lips against his.

Bane ground his mouth over hers but before they could take the next step, they broke apart at the sound of someone knocking on the door.

Chapter Eleven

Growling with annoyance, Bane got to his feet, marched over to the door and yanked it open, ready to smash whoever stood there to mush.

Priest raised an eyebrow and stared at the other man. Then looking beyond Bane, he saw Sarah sitting on the bed with a red face. He chuckled then sobered. "We have to talk."

Bane stood back and allowed the other man into his room.

Sarah got to her feet and brushed her lips with Bane's. "I'll see you later."

When she left, Priest shut the door and walked over to the window looking out over the backyard. Neither man said a word for a number of minutes, then Priest broke the silence by asking, "What's your next move?"

"Excuse me?" Bane asked.

"Where are you going from here?" he repeated his question. "I have a reason for asking."

"And that would be what?" Bane narrowed his eyes at him.

"As you know, I've never trusted my life to many people. With what I did, I couldn't trust anyone but James with my secrets. But that was enough. It was me and him against the whole world. Then I met Sawyer and I wanted her in my life. I didn't know if I could have her with all my enemies but I wanted her. I finally took that chance and I couldn't be happier. I have her and a son now. But there is a desperate need out there and someone has to fill it."

"What need would that be?"

"The need for someone to fight for the underdog. There are great injustices happening every day and it's the little people getting caught up in the muck and the mud left behind. I think you and I could help balance the scales. I think you, me and James can take back the shadows that rule the underworld."

Bane just stared at the other man. Then before he thought about it much he asked, "What makes you think I can do that? I mean you know my past. I was part of that dark underworld. Do you really think I could change that much and work for the underdog instead of the big men with the money?"

Priest nodded. "I think you can do anything you want to do with your life. If you want it bad enough that is." He nodded at the door. "I see you want her bad enough to maybe find your happiness with her."

"I tried to tell her about my past and she didn't want to hear it. She said she fell in love with me and she didn't need to know my past. How crazy is that?"

"She could be very good for you, my friend."

"I've done some pretty bad things in my past and the worst thing was the insane amount of money I collected to kill a man. I didn't know or care if the men I killed deserved death or not. It never mattered before."

"Yet, when your niece needed someone on her side you were there, not once but twice. You were there for her, even if she didn't know it was you this time, you wouldn't leave her future to the fates."

Bane shook his head. "I think she knows it's me. She saw it in my eyes. She may not want to believe it but she knows I was here for her."

"That could be a good thing." Priest nodded.

"So this plan of yours, what would it all entail?"

"We could set up shop anywhere you want. I have a few home bases all over the states and a few cases we could start with. Like you, my past often comes to knock on my door and I know secrets no man would be comfortable me knowing. I've hidden my identity as well as I could but there are bound to be people out there that would be willing to take a chance looking for me. To right some past wrong. I know I can take care of myself in any situation but now I have a wife and a family to take care of too. With them, I feel anything is possible, with them I know I can do this, but that's not the real reason I want this so much."

"Then what is?" Bane asked.

"I think it is because of them that I want this so much. Sawyer hasn't had a good life, because of a man her mother never got her happy ever after. And Sawyer almost paid the ultimate price for someone else's choices. I know the need is out there for our services and I want to spend the rest of my life giving people a real choice."

Bane walked closer to the window and shared the view with Priest.

For a moment, neither man said a word. Instead, they shared the silence comfortably.

"Before I agree to this, I want first say on our first job."

"Ok, lay it out for me."

"I want to bring hell down on Sarah's uncles. Her stepfather almost killed her mother and she killed him to save her mother's life. I want his brothers to pay for the fear she's lived with for the last twelve years."

"I'll be happy to do that job. Vengeance will be ours," Priest swore under his breath.

"No, vengeance will be mine," Bane stated. He turned to Priest and held out his hands. "To our new adventure."

"To Vengeance Is Mine." Priest grinned. "We're gonna kick some serious ass brother."

Bane nodded. "Together, we can do anything we need to do to safeguard our families."

~*~

Pappy looked up as his sister joined them in the main room. He smiled as she made her way over to him. "Sadie, how are you?"

Sarah blushed. "I haven't heard that name in so long, I almost forgot it was mine."

Pappy smiled. "You know you'll always have a home with me if you want it right?"

"Even though I lied all those years ago?"

Pappy smiled softly. "I understand why you did that, I can forgive those lies, just don't make a habit of it." He wrapped her in his arms and held her for a moment.

When he let her go, she stepped back and waited.

"Now we have to talk about the man you're with." He nodded at her.

Sarah held her hand over his mouth. "Please, I know what you think. You think I've been running for so long I don't know what I want anymore. But I do know, I do know what makes sense for me. I may not know everything about Theo but I do know that I need him, that I love him. And I will always love him. He takes very good care of me."

"But taking care of someone is different than really loving them," Pappy argued.

Sarah smiled. "I know that. I don't love him because he takes care of me. I love him because he makes me feel loved. He gives me everything I ever wanted. He makes my heart skip a beat every time he enters the room. When he holds me I feel butterflies in my soul."

"And now?" Pappy asked. "Where do you go from here?"

"I'll go wherever he takes me."

"Well, I expect to hear from you wherever you end up and if you ever need me just pick up a phone and call me. I'm there for you now too. I don't want you to disappear on me again. When the Connors are taken care of, I'm moving mom closer to me in Texas. She won't have to hide anymore either." He nodded. "Maybe she can finally have the kind of life she deserves too."

"I hope so. I really hope so," Sarah whispered.

~*~

Deke walked over to where Breaker and Amy were sitting. He sat down at their table and nodded at Amy. Then he looked at Breaker. "Are you all right man?"

Breaker shook his head. "I left this MC to have a life with a woman I loved. I got the life I wanted but there was always something missing you know. I mean I loved Katie and our life together and I love this kid even more." He nodded at Amy. "But now I can't go back to that life. She's not there anymore. I can't go forward either."

"Well, you're welcome to stay here until you figure things out," Deke offered.

Breaker's shoulders slumped. "Thanks man, I appreciate that. I don't know what I want to do just yet but with some help I know I'll figure it out." He looked over at his daughter. "I know I want the best for her though."

"Dad, I'll be fine as long as we're together. You should know that." She looked around the room. "And I could totally live here. I don't think I could go back to Concord without Mom waiting for us."

Deke grinned. Getting to his feet, he held out his hand. "Welcome back brother."

Breaker grinned and shook Deke's hand.

Epilogue

Bane slipped out of the clubhouse. There was still one thing he had to do before he could move on. Falling back into a lifetime's habit, he kept to the shadows as he made his way to her house. He should avoid her. He knew he should since she'd recognized him but he had to see her one more time before he left for parts unknown.

He stood in the shadows of her house. Like a stranger peeking in a window observing her life, he saw her moving around her home. She was preparing a meal and he watched her for a long moment.

Then he heard someone stepping up behind him. "Who are you and what do you think you're doing here?" a child demanded of him.

Bane slowly turned around to face the young boy standing there. He was young, maybe seven or eight years old. His hair was a little longer than Bane liked but it looked good on him. The light brown color was sun faded. Bane gasped at the boy's eyes. They looked a lot like his Grace's eyes.

Suddenly, the boy called out, "Aunt Cricket, can you come out here for a minute?"

A moment later, the back door opened and Cricket stepped out of her kitchen. "Dusty, what the heck?" Then she noticed the taller man standing in the shadows. She grabbed Dusty and hauled him away from Bane. "What are you doing here?" She glared at him.

"I had to see you, just once," Bane told her.

"Do you know this guy, Cricket?" Dusty glared as he looked between Bane and his aunt.

Cricket nodded. "Can you go check on the kids for me Dusty? I don't like to leave them alone too long."

"Sure, I can do that." He gave Bane a long hostile look. "He isn't gonna hurt you is he?"

Bane shook his head. "No, I would never hurt your aunt."

Dusty gave him one more glare then disappeared into the house.

"How are you still alive?" Cricket demanded. "I was told you were shot in the face. They could barely recognize you."

"Obviously that man wasn't me," Bane replied. "I was there and I blew up the clubhouse with Stark inside. But when I thought the threat was over I began climbing down from my tree and as I was walking away Stark found a way out of the fire. He got a shot off before I could turn around and take his miserable life. His bullet caught my shoulder from the back. It was a through and through. I walked deeper into the woods and I could feel the blood soak my clothing. I found a tree and sat down when I couldn't walk any more. My thoughts that night were something I never took the time to think about before. I thought about your parents."

"My parents?" Cricket questioned. "Why were you thinking about my parents?"

"I was also thinking about you. How you were a combination of the both of them. You had your mother's tenacity and your father's strength. You were soft yet stubborn just like my Grace had been. You had the street smarts Orrin had and the common sense he had. It was rare to find both of those traits in one person. Usually, one is common but not both. But you were so much more than just a clone of your parents. You had grit, real honest grit. You called it honor but it was so much more than that."

"Why are you still here? Everyone thinks you died a year ago," Cricket asked softly. "I buried you a year ago."

"I know." Bane nodded. "Bane Jessin did die a year ago. He died begging his brother and his wife to forgive him. He died admitting he had been so wrong about them, about his life. Bane Jessin never begged anyone for anything but he begged Grace and Orrin for forgiveness for the way he ruined their lives."

"How did you manage to get out of those woods?" Cricket rubbed her upper arms as if a ghost just walked over her grave.

"A friend was there for me. He helped get me out of there. He set up the body they found that day. He got me to a place I could recover, a place that offered me shelter to change my face, to change the direction of my life and most of all to heal."

Cricket couldn't look at him. "We found your will. We went to your house and we took things from it. Things we didn't know you might want back." Hanging her head, she admitted. "We took your money."

Bane reached out and tipped her eyes to meet his. "Child, it's fine. I wanted you to have that. The money? It doesn't matter."

"Why did you come here tonight?"

"I guess I just wanted to let you know I was still here. You recognized me earlier didn't you?"

Cricket nodded. "I couldn't believe it was you though. I thought I was going crazy for a moment."

Bane nodded. "I wasn't going to say anything but then I was caught." He glanced in her kitchen window. "Was that Dusty? My grandson?"

Cricket grew afraid for a moment. Taking a deep breath she admitted, "Yes that was Dusty. He'll be eight years old soon." She reached out and touched Bane's arm briefly.

When he looked down at her touch, she pulled her hand away and flushed. Looking away, she told him, "He's got a good life here. He's living with his dad and Paige. Paige is good for him and I'm still around. I look after him too. With Gambler, he's got a man in his life that loves him and will teach him everything he needs to know. He's got a little brother or sister waiting to meet him in a few months." She paused and with a sob, she told her uncle, "He's happy here. He's going to school and he has friends. It's not at all like it was when Cordy was alive."

"That seems like a lifetime ago, doesn't it?" he whispered. "My children were too much like me, weren't they? Like the soulless man I used to be."

Cricket didn't say the words instead, she nodded.

"I was offered a do over and I took it. I am a changed man and I intend to make that change. I learned something about myself in the past year. I may not have deep feelings like everyone else but I do have feelings. I found that while I thought I loved your mother I really didn't. I cared for her the best I could when we first met but I never truly loved her. I was an arrogant man back then. And in my arrogance, I thought just because I wanted her I could make her love me. When I couldn't, I didn't know what to do about it. She belonged to me but I couldn't love her, not like Orrin did. Orrin was a better man for Grace. Cordelia and Michael were born from my union with Grace but they weren't born out of love, they were born out of hate. Grace hated me and I can't blame her for that. She hated the man I was back then. And I didn't know how to be any different."

"You said you got a second chance to change your life." Cricket wet her dry lips with her tongue. "Have you? Have you changed any?"

Bane nodded. "As strange as that sounds, I think I have changed. I think for the first time in my life, I've found the way to a softer life, a life filled with color instead of just black and white. A life filled with wonder and beauty and I think I found someone to love me."

"Sarah?" Cricket smiled softly.

"Sarah," he confirmed.

"So now what? What are you going to do with the rest of your life?" she asked.

"I may have a plan for that. We're working on the details yet but it sounds like a plan to me." He paused and looked in her kitchen window again. Looking back at her, he stated, "One day, I would like to meet that young man, maybe not today or tomorrow or next week but one day. I don't expect he needs to know we're related, if that's the way it has to be but I would like to meet him in person."

Cricket nodded. "I'll ask his dad and see if we can set that up." She dared to step forward and look him in the eyes, "I want to wish you well uncle, with the life you've chosen and with Sarah. I hope she can make you happy."

Bane reached out and cupped her jaw. Leaning forward, he brushed his lips on her forehead and stepped back. They both heard a gasp behind him and as they turned, they saw Raine standing there with clenched fists.

"What the hell is going on here?" he asked in a tight voice.

Bane held up his hand to stop the other man. "Nothing at all. I was just saying goodbye to my niece, that's all."

Raine frowned. "Your what?"

Cricket stepped over to Raine and whispered something in his ear.

Raine's eyes widened as he stared at the other man.

Bane stared back at Raine and after a minute, he said, "I hope we can keep this between the three of us. I have too many enemies that would bring hell to this place if they knew I was still alive. I died in the woods a year ago, please let Bane Jessin stay dead. For everyone's sake."

With those words, he turned and walked away, swallowed by the ever growing shadow of the darkness.

~*~

Raine turned to his wife and gathered her in his arms.

Cricket snuggled in the arms of the only man she could ever love. Her past had a way of popping up when she least expected it to. It wasn't all bad but she still longed for the day when it would just go away. She had enough of Cordy's lies and pain, enough of Michael's bullshit and now she finds out her uncle was still alive.

All she ever wanted was what she found with Raine, nothing more than that and nothing less. He and their children and Dusty were enough for her. Maybe Bane could live another type of life, she hoped so and she hoped Sarah would be everything her mother hadn't been to him. She secretly wished him well. Then she turned to her husband and kissed him wildly in the dark. "I love you husband," she whispered wickedly in his ear.

"I love you too, wife," Raine told her as he nipped her earlobe.

Then Cricket squealed and ran toward the backdoor with Raine hard on her heels...

Note from K.J. Dahlen

K.J. has a new plot in mind. With series name of Vengeance Is Mine If you would like to see this new series with Bane, James and the Priest... Please say so in a review at the retailer you purchased it from or come and post your opinion in her Facebook group>>>

<u>K.J. [1]Dahlen's[2] reader group[3]</u>

---

1. https://www.facebook.com/groups/1538834079503734/

2. https://www.facebook.com/groups/1538834079503734/

3. https://www.facebook.com/groups/1538834079503734/

Excerpt From The Next KJ Dahlen Release
At All Costs
(Aries)
Whiskey Bend MC Series

Chapter One

The ringing phone woke Luna Mathias from a sound sleep. On the third ring, she groaned. Reaching out, she picked up the receiver and whispered a sleepy, "Hello."

"I have received the payment you promised." She heard someone say. "By this time tomorrow, your judicial troubles will be over, the only witness will be dead, and you'll be in the clear."

Luna frowned and sat up in bed slowly. She brushed her long dark hair away from her face and rubbed her eyes. She'd been so tired lately, she wasn't sure she was hearing the conversation correctly. "Excuse me?" She took a deep breath. "Who is this?" When she heard no reply she asked, "Is this some kind of joke or something? Because if it is, this isn't very funny."

She heard a sharp intake of breath and a muffled swear word then she heard a resounding click as the phone call ended. She frowned and reached over to snap on the bedside lamp. Hanging up the phone she glanced at the alarm clock sitting on the bedside table and saw it was just after two a.m.

She hated phone calls in the middle of the night. They never brought good news, only bad news and this one sounded like a prank call. Yet, something she heard in the caller's voice made her stop and think.

It could have been a prank call or something a little more sinister. As a small-town reporter, her inner alarms were going haywire. She knew this sort of thing happened all the time and yet, she had been shocked by the phone call. This sort of crime, a murder for hire, was more a big city occurrence, it didn't happen so much around here. Whiskey Bend may have its own share of crime but it was still a small town and nothing like this happened here. The caller had sounded very sincere about what he was planning to do. In the small amount of conversation she had with the caller, she could sense his intent. If she believed him, someone or maybe more than one someone would die in the next day.

Luna shivered. She'd just spent the last three days trying to track down a serial killer. She had seen too much death since she began this quest. She received a call four days ago from an attorney for a man on death row. The attorney had said his client's name was Mike Denver and he was dying of cancer. Mike knew he wouldn't live long enough to get the needle and he felt okay with that. The attorney informed her Mike had a story to tell, and he wanted her to tell it. He told her she had every right to refuse, it was okay if she wanted to turn around and walk away. He would understand, but he hoped she would at least listen to his story.

Luna had been just curious enough to stay. Mike wanted to tell her about someone he met fifteen years ago in Detroit. He'd recently read a story she wrote about child abuse and he told her he liked the way she brought the victims to life. That she made him feel the child's pain and when she was finished, he felt that justice had been done by the courts. He felt the judge who sentenced the couple to prison had stopped them from hurting any other child. He wanted the world to know his story and why he had done the things he had done. He wasn't looking for forgiveness; but he did want people to know what he felt during the time he was committing his crimes. While he'd done a number of bad things in his life, he needed to tell the world about a man that scared even the hardest of criminals.

As a reporter, even a small town reporter she knew this man had a story to tell and she told him if she could verify what he was telling her, she would write his story. What she found out scared the hell out of her, but she had been able to verify his tale in New York, Chicago, Seattle and St. Louis; and many little towns along the way. What she never told anyone, the child in her abuse story was herself.

She had returned from her journey only three hours ago. Her suitcase was still sitting just inside the bedroom door. All she wanted to do when she got home was sleep.

Luna grabbed a pen and a notepad she kept close to her and wrote down the message she had been given. She knew she should call Charlie Boone, but if she did and it turned out to be a crank, she didn't want to look like a fool in his eyes. The caller had said that the hit would happen within twenty-four hours. The question was who was going to die and why? The reporter in her wanted to know the five W's; who, what, when, where and why. So far, she knew the when but she didn't know the rest. She tried to think of upcoming interesting cases, but she couldn't think of one that would warrant this kind of solution. This was Whiskey Bend after all. Being the seat of Bison County there was a courthouse located here, as well as a jail. The DA and judge lived here too.

Her adrenalin was pumping and she knew from the butterflies in the pit of her stomach she had stumbled on to a story that she was never supposed to know about. What she would do next might save someone's life or cost her own.

She got up and walked over to the window. Pulling the drapes open, she stared out at the town beyond her windows. Even in the darkness, she could see her neighborhood. She knew by heart every inch of what lay beyond her window. She was part of the neighborhood watch, although here in Whiskey Bend people tended to watch over one another and she knew her neighbors as well as they knew her. The streetlights shone at every corner illuminating the yards and houses nearby. Down the street from where she lived, there was a Catholic church and a public school. During the day, the people bustled along doing their own thing but it was basically a safe town, a good town to live in and raise a family. Had the horror of the big city finally come to Whiskey Bend, Wisconsin? Luna shivered as the cool night air blew in from her open bedroom window.

~*~

In a small room in a rented cabin just outside Whiskey Bend, a man was sitting in the dark. The neon sign across the road flashing a beer sign gave him more than enough light to dial a phone. He hadn't thought about turning his own lights on until now. Before he could snap the light on, the flashing sign across the street went out for the night. Getting up, he moved over to the window and looked outside. The parking lot across the street was finally empty after being full earlier. The music that blared earlier was gone as well. Everything was quiet now, except his mind. His mind was going crazy with the mistake he'd just made. Now he would have to find and eliminate the witness he might have just informed of his intentions.

He always used a motel or a cabin such as this one for his business. That way, the cops couldn't trace any of the calls back to him. He also used a false name and a disguise to register at the motel. He didn't want anyone to know his true identity. After all, he had his own reputation to protect, as well as his day job. Every time he had to do a job, he would use a different hotel or motel in the area. If the police ever thought to trace the incoming and outgoing calls made by the people who hired him, all they would find was a person they could never trace. And a series of untraceable burn phones as he bought a new trac phone for every job he did. It kept him clear of any suspicion in the cases and it gave his clients some protection as well. He wasn't exactly a rookie at police work or his sideline. He gave both of his occupations his full attention to detail and so far, neither one had crossed over into the other.

He looked at the phone sitting on the table and frowned. The numbers on the piece of paper were the same numbers he had dialed, yet his contact had sounded like a woman. He reached over and flipped on the light. He checked the numbers again and hit the redial. The number he had dialed flashed and when he looked at it he realized he had switched two of the numbers around. It was a common mistake except he couldn't afford to make *common* mistakes.

He growled as he quickly wrote down the number he had called and slammed the phone down. "Damn, I got the wrong number." He paused to light a cigarette. As the smoke circled his head, the man again looked at the number on the paper. This time he dialed it correctly and when his contact answered the call, he repeated his earlier message.

"Are you sure you can handle this job?" his contact asked again. His voice was a little on the high side and it had a certain whiney quality.

"Do you want the job done or not?" he asked his contact. "I mean it doesn't matter to me whether they are dead or not, but once you pay, I do the job. I don't do refunds if you change your mind."

The contact scoffed. "I don't want a refund, I want the job done. I want Sheila Donner dead. The little bitch thinks she can blackmail me. I'll show her I won't be blackmailed by anyone."

"Hey man, I don't need to know the details," he told the contact. "In fact, I don't want to know the details." His voice had grown cold. "I just called to inform you that the money was delivered."

"Ok, ok. I understand and I'll be ready."

He hung up without saying anything more. There were times when he didn't much care for the people he worked for. Some, like this man, regarded him as nothing more than dirt on their shoes and they tended to treat him as such. He deeply resented them. They all thought they were better than he was, but without him they all would be rotting in some stinking jail somewhere. His only saving grace was that his clients didn't know who he was. To them he was a voice on the other end of a phone call. They couldn't even tell the police what his voice sounded like since his voice was often disguised. All the contact they had was over the phone. To them he was just a phone call away. He could be standing right next to them and they wouldn't know it.

He poured himself another drink from the bottle of Black Velvet sitting on the table. He lit another cigarette and thought about how his life of crime began, so many years ago. He'd lived a lifetime since then, or maybe several life times. His lips curled in some sense of a smile and he contemplated his life. He was a very intelligent man, He had to be. His freedom depended on it. His eyes caught sight of the tattoo on the inside of his right wrist. He had put her face there as a reminder and every time he looked at her he remembered what she did to make him the man he was today. He flexed his thumb and her face changed. It became the face he saw the day he killed her. That day her face had been twisted in hate and she became the monster inside him. She hadn't died easily that day but he held her close to him until he no longer heard her breathing. Then he carefully laid her on the ground and walked away. He hadn't looked back as there was nothing left for him there. His mother was dead and he was truly alone in this world.

Every time he had to start over, he changed his name and profession in another city or town. There had been so many different lives already, he could barely remember his given name anymore.

He stared at the second number on the piece of paper. He got up, grabbed the paper and his drink, then walked over to the laptop computer on the desk. He'd brought it with him tonight so he could get some work done while he was away from home and now he was glad he had. Logging on to his work computer, he quickly entered the information and waited while the reverse directory did its work. In a few minutes, he had the information he needed.

The phone number belonged to a Luna Mathias. He frowned when he realized he knew that name. The DMV photo he was looking at also gave her current address. He sat back in his chair and gazed at the computer screen for a moment. He took another drag from his cigarette and sip of his whiskey as he stared at the information on the screen. As he exhaled the smoke, he leaned forward and hit a few more keys. He thought about where he knew the name from, and he realized according to the information on the screen she was a reporter for the Whiskey Bend Happenings newspaper. Her driver's license photo popped on the screen and he found himself looking at someone else he had to kill before this was all over. This hit was on him as he couldn't afford to leave any potential witnesses behind. He liked this city and he wasn't ready to leave just yet.

She was a loose end he'd created and it was in his best interest to tie up any and all loose ends. He wouldn't be in business very long if anyone knew about what he did. His day job was risky enough. Being a cop in any town, big or small, was a risk these days and even though he didn't live and work in a big city like New York or San Francisco, the town they lived in was a small town. It had barely a thousand people living here and a good deal of them lived on farms in three directions fanning out behind the town. The fourth side of the river was the Mississippi River. The city limits began on the river's banks.

He snubbed out his cigarette in the ashtray sitting on the desk and sat back in his chair. Cradling the whiskey in his glass, he stared at the computer screen for another minute or so. Her driver's license photo burned into his brain and he knew he would never forget her, even after he killed her.

About K. J. Dahlen

Author of the bestselling, award winning Bratva Brothers and Satan Spawns MC Series...

I live in a small town (population 1,000) in Wisconsin. From my deck, I can see the Mississippi River on one side and the bluffs, where eagles live and nest on the other side. I live with my husband Dave and dog Bella. My two children are grown and I have two grandchildren. I love to watch people and that has helped me with my writing. I often use people I watch as characters in my books and I always try to give my characters some of my own values and habits.

I love to create characters and put them in a troubling situation then sit back and let them do all the work. My characters surprise even me at times. At some point in the book, they take on a life of their own and the twists and turns they create becomes the story. Of all the stories I could write, I found I like mystery/thrillers the best. I like to keep my readers guessing until the very end of the book.

Join K.J. [1]Dahlen's[2] reader group[3]

---

1. https://www.facebook.com/groups/1538834079503734/

<u>Newsletter</u>[4]

---

2. https://www.facebook.com/groups/1538834079503734/

3. https://www.facebook.com/groups/1538834079503734/

4. https://confirmsubscription.com/h/j/C38BC78874901A2F

Don't miss out!

Visit the website below and you can sign up to receive emails whenever Kj Dahlen publishes a new book. There's no charge and no obligation.

https://books2read.com/r/B-A-OQCH-LSRV

BOOKS 2 READ

Connecting independent readers to independent writers.

Did you love *Bane*? Then you should read *Spawn & Spitfire*[5] by Kj Dahlen!

The book that started it all....

Spawn and Spitfire

Deke

He's the President of the Satan's Spawn MC. Not because he wants it but because he's earned it.

When he met her, he met his match. His MC dubbed her Spitfire. She didn't fear him like everyone else. Instead, she intrigued him.

He wants to keep her but forces beyond his control don't want that to happen.

He'll do battle with the devil himself to keep her alive and his.

---

5. https://books2read.com/u/mgLd9q

6. https://books2read.com/u/mgLd9q

Because no one messes with what belongs to him and she belongs to him.

Cassie

She didn't come looking for trouble but she didn't run away from it either.

He was the first man she ever met that she wanted more from.

She wants a happy ever after but doesn't know how to get it.

Her past comes looking for her and finds her, can she fight to survive it?

When the battle comes to her it is more than test of wills... this is her forever, can she and Deke survive it?

Also by Kj Dahlen

Badass Women
Badass Women-Savaged Sous MC
Badass Women-Sin's Bastards
Badass Women#3 Brothers Of Chaos
Badass Women-Bratva Blood Brothers
Badass Women-Lost Sons MC
Badass Women VIM
Badass Women-Bratva New York

Bikers Of The Rio Grande
Rambler
Hunter
Sinner
Bearcat
Wizard
Raven
Taz
Thunder
Thunder & A Little Bit Of Lightning
Snowman & Eden

Born Of Desperation
Nitro
Pagan
Repo
Typhoon
Montana
Capone
Dixon

Bratva Blood Brothers
Yuri
Mikial
Barshan
Sazon
Roman
Brothers United
losif
Kosta
Nikoli
Nicky
Sergi
Misha
Timor
Felix
Kirill
Sasha
Maxim, A Bratva Christmas
A Bratva Christmas
Mikial-Father's Day

Valentines-Bratva
Sergi's Father's Day
Bratva Blood Brothers Thanksgiving

Bratva Born
Nubric
Koyla
Petrov
Minki
Dima
Catch
Bratva Women-Prequel-Bratva Born

Bratva Enforcers-Nomads
Viktor
Ivan
Adrik
Andrey
Grisha
Matvey

Bratva New Orleans
Bratva New Orleans#1
Bratva New Orleans#2
Bratva New Orleans
Bratva New Orleans#4

Bratva New York
Nikoli Bratva New York
Misha-New York
Nicky-New York
Felix-New York
Kirill Bratva New York
Sergi Bratva New York
Bratva New York
Christmas-Bratva New York
Crimson- Special Edition

Brothers At Arms MC
Zeus
Diabolus
Memphis
Grave Digger
Click
Captain

Cajun Kings
Cajun King
Fat Tuesday
Born In Fahyuh
Crazy As Hell
Sweet Rascal
I Don't Give A Damn

Cajun Queens
Cajun Queens
Cajun Queens#2
Cajun Queens #3
Cajun Queens #4
Cajun Queens #5
Cajun Queens#6

Crimson Tide MC
Tracker
Boomer
Cyrus
Clovis
Vance
Tether
Crimson Tide MC

Destiny Meets Fate
Destiny Meets Fate
Destiny Meets Fate#2
Destiny Meets Fate#3
Destiny Meets Fate
Destiny Meets Fate
Destiny Meets Fate #6
Destiny Meets Fate Set

Devil's Advocates MC
Jackal
Beast
Wolf
Apollo
Shade
Tank
Shadow Hunter
Devil's Advocates Series Set

Devil's Own MC
Stormy

Devils Trifecta MC
Gage
Joker
Sledge
Devil's Trifecta MC Set

Fire And Ice
Fire And Ice
The Flame
Invincible
Supernatural
Incandescent
Extraordinary

Ghost Riders MC
Pepper
Phantom
Dax
Venom
Heathen
NiteStalker

Hell's Bloodhounds MC
Barron
Leonid

Hell's Fire Riders
A Hell's Fire Christmas

Hell's Fire Riders MC
Pappy's Shadow
Betrayed
Trigger The Storm
Shay
Legend
Birth Of Hells Fire Rider
Trudy

Kings Of Wrath MC
Pride
Candyman
Rage
Scar
Romeo
Cosmos
Kings Of Wrath
Kings Of Wrath Christmas

Lords Of Hell MC
Mayhem
Brutus
Bear
Stone
Tag
Svante

Lost Sons MC
Creed's Return
Jack
Tate
Harry
Silas
Daniel
Silas & Midge
Come Home-Lost Sons MC
Lost Sons MC

Louisiana Heat
Ajax
Fireball
Stinger
Moon
Racer
Player
LA Heat Series

Malverde
Malverde
Malverde 2
Malverde 3

Masters Of Mayhem MC
Rance
Bull
Korbel
Rocker
Nova
Ram

Misfits Of Whiskey Bend
Misfits Of Whiskey Bend

New Blood-Savaged Souls MC
Arrow
Beau
Hayes
Runner
Acer
Duke
New Blood Savaged Souls-Boxed Set

Payback
Ghoster

Phantom Fury MC
Shilo
Bullet

Princes Of Hell MC
Talon
Rogue
Falcon
Condor
Princes Of Hell MC Set

Reunion Series

Reunion
Silk & Bones Reunion
Hell's Fire Riders Reunion
Yuri Bratva Blood Brothers Reunion
Rogue's Of Hell MC-Reunion
Reunion Sin's Bastards MC- Next Generation

Rivers Foundation
Cade

Rogues Of Hell MC
Titan
Kota
Brute
Nash
Wanderer
Hawkins
Rogues Of Hell MC Set
Rogues Christmas

Rogues Of Hell MC Trilogy
Cash

Rogues Trilogy
Wilder

San Francisco Steel
Slammer
Shotgun
Grinder
Mammoth
Booker
Spider
Texas

Satan's Spawn MC
Spawn & Spitfire
Revenge and Retribution
Babies & Bastards

Savaged Souls MC
Boone
Gunner
Jett
Cobra
Thor
Gypsy
Grizzly
Moose
Skeeter

Shades of Shay Trilogy

Shades Of Shay
Shades Of Shay
Shades Of Shay

Shadow Warriors
Blue

Silver Warriors
The Quest
The Ride
The Brothers
The Game
The Fall
The Race
Coming Home
Silver Warriors-Boxed Set
Silver Warriors Halloween

Sinners MC
Hawk
Pony
Prosper
Saber
Rebel
Buzz
Sinners- Boxed Set

Sinners Of Boston
V-Sins & Sinners
Atlas
Echo
Cuffs
Ringo
Dak

Sin's Bastards MC
Silk & Bones
Karma's Bite
No Regrets
Hell's Fury
Lies & Liars
Stone Cold
Sin's Bastards Christmas
Leon
Mountain
Peaches & Iceman
Girl's Night
Sin's Bastards Mother's Day
Bane Returns
Christmas With The Sin's
Deacon
Reva

Sin's Bastards Next Generation
Raine

Chance
Gambler
Bowie
Judge
Byron
Hound
Dante
Iceman
The Kids
Wiley
Calderone
Sin's Bastards MC Next Generation Boxed Set #1
Vincinti Women
Sin's Bastards Next Generation Boxed Set #2
Jericho's Christmas

Soldiers Of Hades MC
Cottonmouth
Python
GTO
Lightning
Whiskey
Spirit
Cobra's New Year
Soldiers Of Hades Christmas

Sons Of Ireland
Sons of Ireland-Boston#1
Sons Of Ireland

Stone Cold Bitches MC
Calypso
Widowmaker
Aqua Velvet
Medusa
Razor
Ruby Red
Stone Cold Bitches MC Set

Swamp Patriots
Swamp Patriots

Tennessee Breeds
Breed
Greer
Monster
Crow
Maverick
Cowboy
Blade
Tennessee Breeds Set

The Boondocks
Mad Dog
Stroker

Vengeance Is Mine
Bane
Damon
Bane's Shadow
Cane
The Priest
Kill Me Twice
Kill Me Again
Lionheart
Lancelot
Galahad
PenDragon
Excaliber
Palamedes
Calegis
Escalades
Theo
Hell's Vengeance
Archangel
Butterfly
Blue Eyes
Dante's Inferno
Conquest
Apocalypse
Poison
Into The Black
White Noise
Absolute
Doom
Faith
VIM Set

Bane's Infinity
Valiant
VIM #2

VIM Redux
VIM Redux

Vincintis
The Vincintis
The Vincintis#2
The Vincintis#3
The Vincintis#4

WarLords MC
Truman
King
Jack- WarLords
Deuce
Joker
Traven
Giving Thanks-Warlord MC

Whiskey Bend MC Series
Lucifer's Woman
Demon's Stand
At All Costs

Out Of The Shadows
Jinx
Shadow
Cooper
Bender
Saint
Whiskey Bend MC Set
Christmas In Whiskey Bend
Whiskey Bend Easter
Misfits Christmas

Wings Of Fire MC
Maze
Tabor
Sayer
Hellion

Standalone
Hell's Fire MC Series Set
Satan's Spawn & Sin's Bastards Collection
A Life For Luke
Chasing Eve
Saving Sebastian
Shadows Of The Past
Never Forget Me
The Cartouche
A Wrath Is Born
The New Brotherhood
Slade
Zipper

Carson
San Francisco Steel MC Set
Return To Yuri
Patriot
Badass Women-Boxed Set
King Of Pain Vol.#1
King Of Pain Vol.#2
Shades Of Shay Collection
Cobra's Christmas
Cajun Queens Boxed Set